Provoke

Also From Rachel Van Dyken

Liars, Inc.
Dirty Exes
Dangerous Exes

Covet Series
Stealing Her
Finding Him

Bro Code Series
Co-Ed
Seducing Mrs. Robinson
Avoiding Temptation
The Set-Up

Elite Bratva Brotherhood
Debase

The Players Game Series
Fraternize
Infraction
MVP

The Consequence Series
The Consequence of Loving Colton
The Consequence of Revenge
The Consequence of Seduction
The Consequence of Rejection

The Wingmen Inc. Series
The Matchmaker's Playbook
The Matchmaker's Replacement

Curious Liaisons Series
Cheater
Cheater's Regret

An Unlikely Alliance
The Redemption of Lord Rawlings
The Devil Duke Takes a Bride

The London Fairy Tales Series
Upon a Midnight Dream
Whispered Music
The Wolf's Pursuit
When Ash Falls

The Seasons of Paleo Series
Savage Winter
Feral Spring

The Wallflower Series (with Leah Sanders)
Waltzing with the Wallflower
Beguiling Bridget
Taming Wilde

The Dark Ones Saga
The Dark Ones
Untouchable Darkness
Dark Surrender
Darkest Temptation
Darkest Sinner

Stand-Alones
Hurt: A Collection (with Kristin Vayden and Elyse Faber)
Rip
Compromising Kessen
Every Girl Does It
The Parting Gift (with Leah Sanders)
Divine Uprising
A Crown for Christmas

Provoke

A Seaside Pictures Novella

By Rachel Van Dyken

1001 DARK NIGHTS

PRESS

Provoke: A Seaside Pictures Novella
By Rachel Van Dyken
Copyright 2020
ISBN: 978-1-970077-90-2

Published by 1001 Dark Nights Press, an imprint of Evil Eye Concepts, Incorporated

Cover photo credit © Annie Ray/ Passion Pages

Sign up for the 1001 Dark Nights Newsletter
and be entered to win a Tiffany Key necklace.

There's a contest every month!

Go to www.1001DarkNights.com to subscribe.

**As a bonus, all subscribers can download
FIVE FREE exclusive books!**

One Thousand and One Dark Nights

Once upon a time, in the future…

*I was a student fascinated with stories and learning.
I studied philosophy, poetry, history, the occult, and
the art and science of love and magic. I had a vast
library at my father's home and collected thousands
of volumes of fantastic tales.*

*I learned all about ancient races and bygone
times. About myths and legends and dreams of all
people through the millennium. And the more I read
the stronger my imagination grew until I discovered
that I was able to travel into the stories… to actually
become part of them.*

*I wish I could say that I listened to my teacher
and respected my gift, as I ought to have. If I had, I
would not be telling you this tale now.
But I was foolhardy and confused, showing off
with bravery.*

*One afternoon, curious about the myth of the
Arabian Nights, I traveled back to ancient Persia to
see for myself if it was true that every day Shahryar
(Persian: شهريار, "king") married a new virgin, and then
sent yesterday's wife to be beheaded. It was written
and I had read, that by the time he met Scheherazade,
the vizier's daughter, he'd killed one thousand
women.*

Something went wrong with my efforts. I arrived in the midst of the story and somehow exchanged places with Scheherazade — a phenomena that had never occurred before and that still to this day, I cannot explain.

Now I am trapped in that ancient past. I have taken on Scheherazade's life and the only way I can protect myself and stay alive is to do what she did to protect herself and stay alive.

Every night the King calls for me and listens as I spin tales. And when the evening ends and dawn breaks, I stop at a point that leaves him breathless and yearning for more. And so the King spares my life for one more day, so that he might hear the rest of my dark tale.

As soon as I finish a story... I begin a new one... like the one that you, dear reader, have before you now.

Prologue

"Hey, guys! It's Braden the musical musician, hitting you up from my home in Portland, Oregon!" I made a little drum sound effect with my keyboard and then added in my normal cymbal. "And here's the thing. I've been getting a lot of requests on my YouTube channel for something sexy. But, guys, I mean…have you seen my hair?" I pointed to my red hair and shook my head. "Told my mom I was gonna dye it, and she told me if I did, then I would, in fact…" I gave an exaggerated gulp and hit a low key on the keyboard. "Die."

I made a slicing motion across my neck and grinned. "Hey, at least I have a nice, strong smile. Thank you, Dr. Pain—his nickname—for letting me wear braces for four years and then saying that one day I'd be at the Grammys dedicating an award to him." I busted up laughing.

"All right, all right." I cleared my throat. "This is as sexy as it gets, ladies. And for all the dudes who have to suffer through this ballad with me, I'm not even sorry because you know you're gonna get lai—"

"Braden!" Mom yelled for me.

I made a face at my computer. "I'm going to be dead if she heard me. Also, hi, Mom. I assume you're watching my live feed. Hey, we're out of Pringles so—"

She stormed into my room, swatted me on the head with an empty can of Pringles, then barreled back out.

"Love you, Ma!" I called over my shoulder.

"Love you too!" she yelled.

I put my hand on my heart. "All right, let's do this."

I had been singing the shit out of my newest song. Within a day of its first airing, it had garnered over two million views. Actually small by comparison to my biggest hit, which had over forty million.

My channel was doing so well that my mom was able to stay home with my little sisters, which just made me feel like the man of the house—I was somehow contributing since my loser dad stopped sending child support eons ago.

I closed up for the night and headed downstairs just as the doorbell rang.

"Braden, can you get that?" Mom said from the kitchen. "I'm elbow-deep in chicken."

"Ew, Mom, take your fetishes elsewhere."

A curse and then, "Braden, I swear I'm going to put naked chickens in your bed if you say something about that on your channel."

I paused for effect and then said. "I'll think about it."

"Braden!"

I busted out laughing as the doorbell rang again. "Hold your ass, man."

I jerked open the door and nearly died when Drew Amhurst, Adrenaline's front man and all-around A-list rock star stood there, sunglasses low on his nose, and both hands on his ass, smirking. "Like this, bro? Or am I doing it wrong?"

I grinned. "Did we just become best friends?"

"I'd shake your hand but you told me to hold my ass."

"Brothers don't shake hands." It totally slipped from my mouth. Before I knew what was happening, Drew charged me, pulled me in for a tight hug, kissed both my cheeks like we were Italian or something, and then set me down.

"Brothers hug."

A side-splitting laugh erupted before I could stop it. I'd only chatted with Drew once when his tour made its way through Portland. He gave me backstage passes since he was a fan of my channel, but that was the extent of our relationship.

"So, any reason my fairy godmother decided to just randomly stop at my apartment? Or were you just out wandering the streets in leather pants, trying to see how many prostitutes offered you drugs out of confusion?"

"Off the drugs." He walked farther into my house and pulled off his aviators. "Thanks, though, for the temptation. I'm actually in the area looking for some wiseass nineteen-year-old who seems to be in competition with our music videos for how many views he can get." He shook his head. "Releasing a live stream the same day we drop our new single? That's cold, man."

I led him into the kitchen and felt my circle of life complete as my gorgeous mom took one look at Drew, then glanced at me, then stared down at her hands all covered in chicken guts before glaring daggers at me like it was my fault the universe was against her.

"Whoa, Mom." I held up my hands. "We've only met once. I did not invite him here to watch you do"—I pointed at the chicken—"whatever it is you do when your hands are all...inside."

She squeezed her eyes shut and gritted her teeth.

"I think she's mad, bro," Drew whispered.

"Shit, I think she heard you," I said right back.

"Braden." Mom took a deep breath, the same type she often took whenever she was getting ready to scold my ass. "What's going on?"

"Oh, I can answer that." Raising his hand, Drew nodded.

"Put your hand down. This isn't school," she said through clenched teeth.

"Bummer." Drew grinned. "Because you would be a great teacher, you know, forming the minds of the youth."

"Isn't it youths?" I interjected.

"Is it?" Drew wondered out loud.

"HOW!" Mom yelled, making both of us jump. "How are there two of you?"

I frowned. "Mom, his hair is brown, so unless you and the guy in the meat department at Safeway had a meaty fling—"

"Ha." Drew snorted. "Good one."

"Never mind." She waved a chicken-gut-covered hand in the air. "Why is a famous rock star in our dirty apartment?"

"Ah..." Drew wrapped an arm around me. "We want him. Actually, my manager Will wants him to sign. My best friend Ty wants to sign him. I mean, basically everyone wants him. But I called dibs because I need help finishing our comeback album."

"Whoa." I looked up at him. "Really?"

"Really, really." Drew nodded. "You should probably pack. I have a plane waiting for the morning."

I whistled. "Not a car but a plane?"

"LA." Drew shrugged. "You can come back on Sunday. It's only two days. You won't miss any classes."

Screw classes. I was a sophomore in college with a rock god in my kitchen.

"Wait. This is—this is crazy. People don't just—" Mom started to pace. "I mean, aren't there contracts and things to—?"

Drew dropped a black portfolio on the counter. "Once you've cleaned up—not that you need to," he added quickly, "look this over. I'll be back in the morning to grab Braden. He can still do all his YouTubing. We have a signing bonus from the production company, and if it all works out—and if it's okay with both of you—Braden's gonna be the first musician I mentor."

I tried not to collapse against the counter.

Mom gaped at both of us. "I...I don't know what to say. Why Braden?"

I shot my mom a don't-mess-this-up-for-us look. Her pretty brown hair was pulled back in a low ponytail, and she wore a mismatched pink apron.

This sort of life could change us.

It would mean more and more money coming in.

It would mean freedom.

And my dreams coming true.

I'd wanted this since I was seven.

Had gotten approached several times at the age of sixteen and had done a few collaborations with some budding artists. I was famous in the YouTube world. But this was beyond that. This was the next logical step in my career, and I wanted it so bad I could taste it.

"We've had our eye on him for a while," said Drew with a half-assed shrug. "Watched some of his collaborations. But honestly, the real reason we waited this long was because getting tossed into this life at such a young age changes you in ways I didn't want for him. Hell, I'm thirty, and I'm still trying to process all the shit we were put through in the name of record sales and money. He just turned nineteen. But after his last few videos went viral, we all sat down and decided we wanted him."

I felt my eyes mist a bit because, damn it felt good to be wanted. And because a small part of me loved that they'd waited, that they understood I wanted to do it right. Although they didn't even know me well enough to know that.

"Okay," my mom said slowly. "We'll look over the contracts tonight and give you an answer in the morning." She sighed, washed her hands, and then grabbed a stack of plates. "In the meantime—" She handed the plates to Drew; the white porcelain looked funny against his black finger tattoos. "Set the table."

Drew laughed.

I elbowed him. "She's dead serious."

"Oh shit." Drew straightened his stance a bit. "Yes, ma'am."

"Fill the water too!" she called as he rounded the corner to the dining room table.

"Right away!"

I snickered. "What? Five minutes in my house, and you think she's a sergeant in the army?"

"She's terrifying," Drew said under his breath. "Kinda hot though for—"

"I wouldn't." I patted his back. "Last friend of mine that hit on her had to sit on frozen peas for weeks."

Drew made a face.

And then we fell into an easy silence before he nodded. "We chose good."

"I won't let you down."

"I know, man. I know."

Chapter One

Braden

Present Day
5 Years Later

I drummed my fingertips against the cold granite counter and nearly jumped a foot when Drew walked into the beach house with one of our mutual rock star friends, Zane Andrews. He took one look at me and whispered, "You sure you're okay?"

"Fine," I answered in a clipped tone, rubbing my hands back and forth in a self-soothing motion that my therapist said would help me focus on something other than the incident.

Because that's what we were calling it.

The Incident.

Actually, no, that's what the superfans were calling it.

I wasn't sure how it actually happened, but it was typical for followers to make up names for themselves. You got the Swifty's, The Army, The Monsters... I mean, the list went on and on. And yeah, I got it. I did. It unified them like our music did to them...ergo, it was their way of connecting in a way that mattered.

And up until last year, I was completely okay with it. Until a senseless shooting ruined everything and loud noises started reminding me of gunshots. Guilt wrapped around me like a heavy, lead blanket.

"He's shaking," Zane pointed out like I wasn't sitting right there on a barstool, staring out across the vast white sand beach of fucking Seaside, Oregon.

I was an hour from home, but it might as well be thousands of miles.

I'd moved my family to LA the minute I knew I couldn't make the commute. Funny how the one place I'd escaped was the only place I could find solitude.

Seaside, Oregon.

I ran my shaking hands through my hair and tried to ignore my friends' concerned looks. Then again, they had a reason to be worried. I'd been practicing with them for the upcoming tour, doing awesome, even thought I was over my debilitating stage fright.

And all it took to bring it all back was one of the lights falling next to me, along with a crazed fan with my name on her shirt, hiding in my dressing room.

I lost it.

Grabbed my guitar and boarded the first private plane I could to Seaside, never looking back.

That was three weeks ago.

And the tour was in sixty days.

Since then, I'd been active on my channel but that was easy, it was just me and my fans. I didn't have to frantically search the audience for weapons because I was staring at a computer screen.

Sixty days. I reminded myself that it wasn't just the guys' careers hanging in the balance, it was mine too. I owed them songs, and I still owed the record company my next album. But how was I supposed to write when my mind was broken?

"Look." Drew pulled out a barstool and sat in front of me. His tattoos looked dark against the white granite as he leaned his massive body against the counter. "If you don't come on tour, you'll be in breach of contract—"

I opened my mouth, only to have him raise his hand.

I jerked my head in a stiff nod.

"We don't want that. AD2 has been dying to tour with you. Our band and you have been inseparable since you broke out on your own a few years ago. And you know Zane cries himself to sleep when you don't sing for him."

"One time," Zane grumbled. "And my wife was away. I was lonely."

"Hug a bear." This from Drew, earning a smack from Zane. "Look, Braden, I'm not saying what happened wasn't horrible. God knows it's not excusable, and I totally get how things might trigger you now, like the light and shit." He sighed. "But you need to move past it. And I think the only way for you to do that is to get back on stage and give the world hope again."

I swallowed the lump in my throat, then shoved away from the chair, taking care to put most of my weight on my *good* leg. My limp was noticeable if I sat too long. My right leg was just tired, but it *was* a constant reminder of the incident.

A nagging reminder.

That I'd had everything.

And in the blink of an eye, a psycho had used my music, my concert, to rip it all away.

I squeezed my eyes shut. "It was my lyrics, guys. My pain that caused this."

"Bullshit," Zane swore. "You didn't make him pick up a semi-automatic weapon, Braden. That was all him, he was insane."

"Yeah," I croaked. "We all have a bit of that inside, don't we?"

"Nope." Drew shook his head. "Not going down that path. Look, I'm glad you're here, Seaside has helped all of us relax. I mean, look at Zane. He used to walk around half-naked holding warm marshmallows in his pocket. Today, he's wearing a shirt."

We both looked at the garment in question. It had at least three gaping holes, and both of us were very aware of a pierced nipple.

Drew winced. "Yeah, bad example. But you get what I mean."

"I don't know." I bit down on my lower lip. "I want it. You guys know how bad I want this, it's the tour of a lifetime. I just...I can't let you down."

"You won't." Drew grinned.

I narrowed my eyes. "I don't like that smile."

"Nobody does," Zane muttered. "He does it on purpose."

"Spill." I eyed Drew. "What did you do?"

A knock sounded on the door.

"Please let that be pizza," I muttered.

"Highly doubt that, bro." Zane slapped me twice on the back. "What Drew wants, he gets, and he wants you to play. Your songs are the reason their last album sold over five million in pre-sales. So just...go with it. Or try."

That was the problem.

I'd been trying.

And I still felt like I was going crazy.

I wasn't sleeping at night.

I couldn't check social media without seeing my name or the incident trending. And I refused to watch the news.

Too much hatred.

Too much sadness.

Too many shots of my shell-shocked face and bandaged leg.

A woman in her early twenties walked into the room and hugged Drew. She had on a black pencil skirt and a tuxedo jacket that looked as if it belonged in an expensive store. One that I refused to shop at because spending more than fifty dollars for a T-shirt was wasteful.

The soft click of her patent leather heels made it feel like I was getting walked toward the plank, and then her eyes locked with mine.

She had jet-black hair that went past her chin, icy blue eyes, and full, red lips that begged for a man to suck.

I almost asked if they got me an escort.

As if that would cheer me up.

Hell, I was losing it. Even the idea of sex with a hot girl made me want to run headfirst into the ocean.

"Braden…" Drew cleared his throat, that creepy damn smile still in place. "Meet Piper Rayne."

I hesitated for a minute and then held out my hand.

One arched eyebrow lifted before she shook.

I ignored the weird pulse between our palms and simultaneously wondered how Drew would feel if I just bolted out the window.

Our hands dropped.

I cleared my throat. "Do you, uh, work for the band?"

"Management," she said in an almost robotic tone. "Okay, gentlemen, I think I'll take things from here. We'll see you in a few weeks."

It was then that I noticed her suitcases—plural—at the door to my rented beach house.

"Wait." I grabbed Zane, only to have him give me a panicked look that said *you're on your own.*

"Drew!" I clenched my teeth. "What the hell, man?"

"Desperate times call for desperate measures, and she's the best. You have twenty-one days to get him ready to tour."

"We'll be fine," she said smoothly.

"Look, lady, no offense." I held up my hands. "But I don't know you, and you sure as hell aren't staying in my house with your giant Louis Vuitton luggage and condescending attitude and—"

"Contract," Drew interrupted. "It states in your contract we're allowed to intervene, and you must exhaust all options before you pull out of the tour."

"Oh yeah?" I sneered, suddenly angry. "And what's she? A shrink?"

"Don't be silly." She smirked. "I'm your new life coach."

I had just enough time to glare at Drew's and Zane's disappearing forms before the door closed with a resounding click.

"I think I'll pass."

"If you do," she informed me with a grin, "you're in breach of contract. Put up with me, and the band won't be forced to sue you. Now where shall I put my bags?"

Rage filled me and affected my vision. "Pick a room."

"Why don't you pick one for me? Oh, and sorry, they're a bit heavy. I'm not a light packer. I'll just go search for some wine. It was a long flight."

And just like that, Piper Rayne, life coach and pain in the ass, invaded my kitchen.

And my life.

Chapter Two

Piper

He looked older than I assumed. I mean, I was nearly twenty-seven, and I knew he was twenty-four, so in my mind, I assumed he'd be this scrawny, just-graduated, college-looking dweeb with a guitar pick stuck between his teeth, a solid subscription to Proactiv, and exactly five hairs on his upper lip that he claimed was his *'stash*.

Not the case.

I took a sip of wine—the guy at least had good taste—and glanced around the large room. I had a balcony that overlooked the ocean, a closet to die for, and even though the room was stark white and a bit bare, I immediately loved it. I wasn't one for lots of knickknacks. I liked solid colors, a good streamline, and Braden's beach house had that in spades.

Braden... Just saying his name in my head reminded me of that firm handshake and the way his red hair fell over his perfectly sculpted face as his lips pressed together in a full line. Why did guys always get the strong jawlines and full lips? I shook my head and took a calming breath. My suitcases were in front of the bed. I knew before I left LA that I'd need to put on a bit of armor since I was working with a younger singer. I just didn't expect...him.

I opened the first suitcase and saw that my black clothes were all still neatly folded.

Black was easy.

It matched at all times.

Was extremely slimming.

Hid stains.

And always looked on point when I was traveling.

Then again, I'd been living out of a suitcase for longer than usual considering the blow-up with my ex-boyfriend. I gritted my teeth then tried to focus on the positive.

New client who just needed to get over some stage fright.

Piece of cake.

I let out a snort just thinking about the poor rock star in the living room with his ginger hair, dimpled smile, many tattoos, ripped, gray T-shirt and distressed jeans.

Did he own any clothing that didn't have holes in it?

Yeah, he was the exact opposite of order and organization.

When my boss called and said that he was tossing me into more celebrity-filled waters, I automatically went into work mode. I wrongly assumed that it would be some actress who needed direction or had a meltdown on set. Maybe an actor struggling through a life crisis, or someone who'd just had enough of the lifestyle and needed a good, solid life plan outside of being told what to do every single second of every single day.

I'd never once in my life dealt with anyone from the music industry. The firm I worked with was private, discreet, and catered to wealthier clients who, after realizing every goal they set out to accomplish, often became depressed with their lives and needed to find direction. A purpose outside of what used to be their passion. And nothing on Earth was more gratifying than witnessing that moment.

It was like a sunset that took your breath away.

The first snow.

Birth.

It was like someone shouting "hallelujah" in the middle of church.

People always talked about the moments in their lives, the ah-ha ones. And lucky for me, I was almost always the one who helped facilitate that with my clients.

It was what I did.

Normally, I loved that part of my job.

Which again brought me back to the present.

How the heck was I supposed to help a singer who'd, if the media was to be believed, had a meltdown on stage after someone used his concert as a way to make a personal statement by way of violence? It didn't help that loud noises triggered him now, and concerts were notoriously loud.

Details were on lockdown.

The media had been oddly quiet about what had actually happened that day, despite all of the video footage. They feared there would be a copycat. And even though Braden had cooperated, he looked a lot different now versus the blurry footage of him on stage.

Haunted.

I'd watched all of his old YouTube videos from when he was nineteen and then graduated to his more recent stuff. He went from looking young to haunted. I wasn't sure what I expected him to be like in person but this wasn't it.

I quickly grabbed my notepad, my duffel bag full of fun, and my notes on the client, then slowly made my way back into the living room.

I could finish unpacking later.

I wanted to get to know Braden first. The *real* Braden, not the one that people saw on TV or worshiped while swaying to his nearly identical Sean Mendes-style voice.

"Braden?" I glanced around the bare-yet-gorgeous living room with its deep brown leather couches, fuzzy white throw pillows, and floor-to-ceiling fireplace.

The doors to the outside folded inside the kitchen. It automatically transported the area into an indoor/outdoor space that had two heaters, an outdoor fireplace, and several fur blankets next to red umbrellas that blocked the wind.

Braden had changed his clothes and was sitting outside with his guitar in his lap, staring out at the ocean. He wore a pair of worn brown Birkenstocks, a black Adidas sweatshirt, black sweats, and a beanie.

I was almost sad his hair was covered.

I'd never seen red hair on a guy that close, and his was like this fiery orange color that looked so shiny and wavy that I imagined it would feel like silk if I ran my fingers through it.

He strummed something on his guitar, a song I wasn't familiar with. I shivered from the cold breeze entering the living room and repeated his name, this time louder.

"Braden?"

He didn't turn around, but he did stop strumming. "Yes, Coach?"

I rolled my eyes, thankful that he couldn't see my irritation. I could put up with a lot, but it would be easier if he wasn't a dick for the next twenty-one days. "I have a name."

He was quiet and then said, "Yes, Piper?" Slowly he turned, his blue eyes locking onto mine with an unnatural intensity, like he could see inside my soul.

I broke eye contact first and walked over to one of the brown wicker chairs. I sat, ankles crossed, posture perfect, lipstick on point. I was well aware that I looked every inch the professional.

Entirely reliable.

I needed to look that way so the clients had faith that if I was in control of myself, I could easily help them gain control of themselves.

I was the spiral stopper.

I lifted my chin and offered a polite smile. "Should we talk?"

His right eyebrow arched as he strummed with his left hand. His fingers were slender and graceful as they moved across the instrument. Why was I fixating on his fingers?

"See something you like, Coach?" He grinned.

I gave him another placating smile. "No, I was just noting that you do that really well."

He barked out a laugh. "You mean strum the chords?"

"Right," I chirped.

His laugh was rich. I liked it immediately. "Look, if you're going to be in my house for the next twenty-one days attempting to fix my brain and life, you should probably relax. Your posture's so rigid, even *my* back hurts, and I do yoga."

"Huh?"

"I have a strong back." He winked. "Normal people slump, by the way. It's a thing."

He went back to playing his guitar and watching the waves crash on the beach.

My smile started to falter. "I don't slump. And your body sends signals to your brain when your posture shows defeat. If you stand straighter, sit straighter, your mind takes notice. Think of it as a way of sending a little alert to your nerves that says, 'Hey, listen up, or look ready for action.'" I could feel my smile growing as I explained the art of body language. I mean, it really was fascinating. "You can even send—"

Braden slumped forward and made a snoring noise, then jerked his head up and laughed. "Did you get that message?"

I glared. "Be serious."

"Hey, you're the one trying to teach. Me being the good student I am, I gave you an example. See? Match made in heaven."

"You were rude."

"Maybe I am rude."

I scowled. "Look, I know you don't want me here, but I promise if you let me do my job, you'll be out there touring in no time. Just think of this as a groupie hiatus if you have to, all right? I'm sorry you're not getting bras tossed at you on stage, and women aren't weeping in your presence right now, but this is going to be like a cleanse to your soul. After me, you're going to feel like yourself again."

His eyes narrowed. "You've never been to one of my concerts, have you?"

I shifted in my seat. "I don't like concerts, they're too loud."

"You're a bucket of fun, aren't you?" Sarcasm dripped from every word.

"What? We all have our things. And I can assure you that I've studied your music extensively, watched your YouTube channel. I've taken notes. I know we can make this work, we just need a plan, and that's where I come in."

His eyes widened. "Didn't think it was possible."

"Making a plan is always possible," I said reassuringly.

He snorted out a laugh. "No, not that. I just didn't think it was possible to actually find someone more terrifying than my therapist, and she doesn't even smile. But you? Your talk of plans and body language and that black duffel bag you creepily have by your feet... Yeah, I'm gonna give you a hard pass. Thanks for trying, but if my own therapist can't cure me of this bullshit, I highly doubt a woman in six-thousand-dollar shoes is going to do any better."

I opened my mouth to say they had been on sale...but then shut it.

"Exactly." He stood. "I'm headed to bed. Sleep tight, Coach, and make sure you lock your door. I get violent when I sleepwalk."

"Wh-what?" I grabbed his file and frantically looked through it. "This says nothing about sleepwalking!" My eyes narrowed. "Are you just being difficult?"

Braden shrugged his massive shoulders. "Better safe than sorry, Doc."

"I'm not a doctor, I'm a life coach."

"So sorry. Better safe than sorry, *Coach*."

I clenched my teeth.

"By the way, the middle two buttons of your blouse have been open this entire time. And well, the wind wasn't helping your situation. I like the pink lace."

With that, he was gone.

And I was clutching my shirt closed as if he'd just seen me naked.

I counted to five.

Breathed in and out.

Grabbed my things and decided to change tactics. I rarely had to force clients to cooperate because they entered into the situation wanting help. Which meant I had to remind Braden why he needed me, and what was at stake if he *didn't* cooperate.

After all, he was the one in danger of being in breach of contract, not me.

Chapter Three

Braden

Day one of Piper taking over my life was going about as well as going to the dentist and having multiple root canals.

Apparently even my breathing pissed her off.

She ordered me to fill out a stack of worksheets that I was one hundred percent convinced would end up sending me to a mental hospital at some point, or at least would come back stating I was crazy.

Then again, you could only fill in so many little circles with a pencil before you wanted to break it in half and then shove it into your thigh to distract yourself from the mental pain of thinking too hard.

"How many more of these, Coach?" I grumbled.

"My name's Piper," she corrected in that same clinical voice that made me want to rip my hair out—and I really liked my hair, so that was saying something. "I need these so I can figure out the best way to help you."

"I don't need help," I snapped, both of us knowing it was a stupid-ass lie but whatever. If I had to fill out one more worksheet...

She was deathly quiet, which was a bit disconcerting since she tended to talk a lot.

Maybe the quiet was what did me in, but I slammed my fists onto the stack of papers and stood. "Look, I know you're here because the company's paying you, and they're scared that they'll have to take me off the tour. But filling out paperwork regarding if I prefer to be alone or in crowds isn't going to fix this. Or me. Or what happened!"

I didn't realize I was raising my voice until she put her hands up and took a step back.

"Shit, I'm sorry. I just…I've been through this, been through the therapy. The breakthrough obviously didn't happen."

She swallowed slowly and then took a few seconds as if she'd either had a stroke or didn't know what to say. "I understand your concerns—"

"See, and that's another thing. I'm a person. Talk to me like a normal human being." I was agitated, annoyed. "You're treating me like some sort of troubled youth, I'm twenty-four." I just had to tell her my age.

"Braden." She said my name softly and then took the stack of papers and shoved them into her briefcase. "I know this is hard, but trust me when I say I'm here to help you. I want to help you. Sometimes it's easier to trust a stranger who's not trying to diagnose you with anything when it comes to trauma and getting over things that make you anxious. Triggers, if you will."

I stared her down. "I feel triggered now, does that help?"

She glared and then forced a smile. "Really? What's triggering you? Because I feel triggered by your poor penmanship."

I looked down. "Bullshit, I write perfectly fine."

"If you were a doctor maybe." She shrugged a shoulder. "So what's setting you off, Braden? The fact that you have to fill out paperwork when you'd rather be writing music? The fact that a stranger's in your home, telling you what to do? What?"

I opened my mouth and then shut it. It was physically impossible not to react to the way she bit down on her bottom lip or looked directly into my eyes like my celebrity status didn't mean shit to her. I was so used to the giddy screams and selfies, that I almost forgot how uncomfortable it was to be so…human.

So normal.

"You," I huffed out. "You trigger me."

"Because I'm a woman?"

I scoffed. "Hell no. My mom would kick my ass. It's because…" A light went on in my head. Shit, was it because I wanted to impress her and I felt embarrassed?

"Because?"

"I like your smile," I blurted. "And I don't like being bossed around by someone who doesn't know the full story of what happened. And I don't like being told what to do. But the biggest trigger of all is that a stunning woman is here trying to help me, and all I keep thinking is, *what if she can't?*"

Her smile was real this time as she pulled out a chair and sat down. "Well, we won't know until we try, right?"

I scowled. "Did you purposely leave out the part where I gave you a nice compliment?"

She licked her lips and looked away. "No. I just didn't want to inflate your head any more by telling you I liked it."

Shock must have shown on my face because she laughed and then eyed the stack of papers.

"So..." I leaned forward. "Does this mean we can be done filling in the holes?" I frowned. "That came out wrong."

"Very," she agreed. "And yes, you can be done filling holes for the day, Braden. I'll go over all of your results while you do what the production company wants you to do."

My ears perked up. "What's that?"

She tossed me a yellow notepad and grinned. "Write."

I went to bed that night with two new songs and a smile on my face. Piper had ordered in pizza, which meant I smelled it first, inhaled five pieces second, yawned and waved goodnight third.

Just because she was hot didn't mean I had to eat with her. Plus, part of me was terrified of letting her in when she was just going to be gone in a few weeks. At least therapists didn't abandon you.

Great. Was I really so pathetic that I was worried about her leaving? Like I had a middle-school crush.

I groaned into my hands and tried to fall asleep, only to realize that I was too damn curious if she was sleeping already or not. Did she wear pajamas to bed? Was she a fan of nude slumber? Should I *check*?

I was screwed.

She was the first woman I'd seen in months that made me go, *yeah, I want to kiss that mouth even though it's attached to someone so prim and proper that I'm worried she'll call me a sinner and knee me in the balls.*

I got out of bed anyway, threw on a pair of gray sweats, and meandered out into the house with a gorgeous woman on my mind. One who had a mouth that liked to give orders rather than receive...anything.

Awesome.

The lights were all low, but the TV was on. She was watching some Netflix documentary I'd seen a few weeks ago, hugging a pillow to her chest, eyes wide.

She didn't even hear me approach until I was next to the couch. "Creepy as hell, right?"

She jumped to her feet with a yelp, knocking over a perfectly good glass of rosé and spilling it across the coffee table.

Holding out my hand, indicating she should remain seated, I stepped into the kitchen, quickly grabbed a towel, and mopped the table clean. As I took one final swipe over the now-dry surface and pitched the rag in the general direction of the kitchen, I made the grave mistake of looking at her.

Because…damn.

She was wearing white linen boy shorts and a matching loose linen tank that most definitely did not hide the fact that she was nipping out.

I gawked and then in a hoarse voice said, "Did you break into my wine stash while I was sleeping?"

Her cheeks blushed bright red. "Maybe?"

"Naughtier than she looks, folks," I teased with a grin. "At least you chose a good one."

"Sorry." She looked sheepish. "I couldn't sleep so I figured it might help. And then my best friend back home was like 'you should watch that cats documentary on Netflix.' And because I'm an idiot, I assumed it was going to be happy, not about cats dying while someone filmed it."

I made a face. "Yeah, not the best thing to watch at night."

"No." She groaned. "I can't stop, though."

I laughed. "Be a little bad. Binge watch the entire season with wine in one hand and mine in the other."

She rolled her eyes. "Cute. You make that up all by yourself, or did you have to write it down and memorize it a dozen times before you got the delivery right?"

I gaped then felt her forehead before pulling back. "Wait, do you actually have a sense of humor?" I slow-clapped. "And here I thought you were half dead. I actually brought salt into my room just in case you turned into some sort of zombie."

"Salt doesn't protect against zombies."

"How do you know?" I asked with a grin.

"Uhhhh." Her eyes narrowed. "You're baiting me."

"Always. I love a good, solid…" I eyed her up and down. "Catch. Hey, question. Are you purposely trying to show me your boobs?"

She crossed her arms. "I thought you were asleep."

"Yeah well, I caught whatever you have, so now I'm up..." And because I was alone, and she was smiling. Because she'd said she could help, and she was, I added in. "Want some popcorn?"

We stayed up until midnight and then went our separate ways. I fell asleep hoping that we'd both decided we were friends of a sort.

Only to find myself woken up the next day by a fucking air horn and another list of likes and dislikes, followed by an assignment to write my own eulogy.

It was a bad day, to say the least.

When I was finished, I tossed the notepad to her and said, "That was bullshit, by the way. And a little too close to home. It could possibly send a person over the edge, so now I'm curious. Why the hell would you make anyone do that?"

"Sometimes..."—she spoke slowly—"it helps to imagine the worst-case scenario and then realize you're here for a purpose. You're here because people need you, and you aren't done with what you're supposed to do on this planet."

I thought about her words throughout a quiet dinner where we barely spoke to one another. And, like the night before, I came out around ten, sat next to her on the couch, and watched more of the documentary.

Wine in one hand, popcorn in the other.

"It should be this easy," I whispered.

"What?" She tilted her head.

"I like this side of you better," I answered instead. "And I'm not telling you how to do your job, but if the Piper sitting next to me right now asked me to bare my soul, I would do it."

"Versus the Piper who's your coach?" she asked.

"She's cold." I shrugged. "You're not."

"I...I don't know what to say to that."

"Maybe it would be easier for both of us if you just crossed the line."

"Make it personal, you mean?"

"Not necessarily. But maybe treat me like I'm a person, not another client on your roster. My heart does beat despite your attempts to get me to want to end my life by way of paperwork."

She smiled. "I'll think about it."

"Good."

Chapter Four

Braden

I went to bed around midnight, my head pounding from all the stupid thoughts running around inside. Like what if she can't help? What if she can? Why do I crave her smile so much, and why do I look forward to the number ten on my watch just so I can eat popcorn with her?

She was all business during the day, driving me insane with her ideas.

But at night? She was mine.

And I liked her better that way, without her armor on, without the red lipstick that seemed more like a deterrent than an invitation.

I quickly shot off a text to Zane, then realized it was a group chat with Will, my agent. Whoops!

Me: FYI next time you guys decide to "help" can you make sure the girl in question isn't Pollyanna with a stick up her ass? Please and thank you.

Will: **Huh? Who are we talking about?**

Zane added Drew, Ty, and Trevor to the conversation.

Well shit, there went the private conversation I'd been about to have.

Zane: **I'll admit she wasn't hard on the eyes. Honest moment, when I heard the term life coach, I imagined some Tony Robins-looking guy in a matching Adidas windbreaker and the inability to use an inside voice, so...**

I frowned at the phone.

Me: Who the hell is Tony Robins?

Trevor: **Ah, youths.**

Ty: **He's loaded, that's what he is. He makes people feel better about being mediocre.**

Drew: **You're just saying that because you're pissed he makes more money than you.**

Zane: **Yeah, he's not wrong. Guy charges more for two days of a convention than a handful of our concert tickets.**

Me: **Wait, back up. He's a life coach?**

Zane: **Keep up, young one. He is, just like her, only she's clearly more...what's the big word I'm looking for? Help a guy out!**

Trevor: **I'll take Rhymes with Concrete for two hundred, Alex!**

Zane: **Discreet! DISCREET. Son of a bitch, why was that hard?**

Ty: **Hard. Just like our poor Braden as the hot life coach kisses his boo-boos and tells him he's not crazy.**

Will: **You're not crazy...by the way.**

Me: **I know I'm not crazy. I'm not the problem. It's all the other psychopaths out there.**

Drew: **Maybe Ty's right. Get laid. It might create more happy chemicals to combat the traumatized ones.**

Me: **Um, he said I was hard, he didn't say to have sex.**

Zane: **Sex fixes everything (said with heavy sarcasm)**

Trevor: **I mean, it can. If you're horny, I guess. But it's probably against her contract to touch you in your happy place.**

Me: **Can we not call it that? Ever? LIKE EVER.**

Zane: **Your fun zone?**

Drew: **Trail of tears?**

Me: **THE HELL?**

Ty: **Because girls weep with pleasure, bro...take a compliment.**

Will: **Yeah, I didn't mean it that way.**

Me: **I hate all of you right now. It's been three days, what if she can't...?**

Will: **She can.**

Zane: **She will.**

Me: **You didn't let me finish.**

Drew: **Look, man, I know you're freaked that she might not be able to help you, but promise us you'll try. I want you touring with** us, all right? You've been family since we picked you up off the streets at nineteen!

Zane: **Sad and wandering in the rain, asking God for a sign.**

Ty: **With an embarrassing amount of Adrenaline and Zane posters in your room.**

Will: **Begging the universe to avenge you!!**

I sighed.

Me: **You guys done? Oh, also, my YouTube video that day got two million MORE views than you guys.**

Drew: **F U. By the way, how's Mom?**

Me: **You're dead to me.**

Will: **To be fair, his mom is really striking.**

Ty: **Not to be creepy or anything but—**

Me: **No, just no. And I'll try, all right? But if she busts out some weird vision board shit, I'm out.**

Zane: **Wait, you don't have a vision board?**

Me: **Tell me you're joking.**

Drew: **His has a pony on it. Don't ask.**

Me: **But why?**

Trevor: **DAMN IT, SOME THINGS DON'T NEED TO BE BROUGHT UP!**

Zane: **lolololololol we'll tell you when you're older, sport.**

Me: **On that creepy note, I need to go shower and head to bed**

Drew: **Taking lots of cold showers, are you?**

Ty: **Hide the socks.**

Trevor: **Out of lotion?**

Me: **I'm flipping all of you guys off. I'm not some pubescent teen. Oh also, I lost my virginity at sixteen and slayed in high school, unlike some people. Cough, cough, Zane.**

Ty: **He was protecting his treasure while you were pillaging every able-bodied female for more.**

Me: **A man doesn't pillage. He does, however, give multiple orgasms. I'll send you a manual later. Sounds like you still need help finding the G spot. It's cool, bro. Not everyone has that skill.**

Drew: **I have that skill in spades.**

Trevor: **We know. We have earplugs because of it.**

Me: **I've never been more proud.**

Will: **Stop setting a bad example!**

Me: **Okay, I really am going, I want to know about the pony** later.

Zane: **You really do. YOU REALLY DO.**

Will: **You'll never be the same, and I mean that. I'm shuddering.**

Me: **I'm out!**

They texted a few more times, and then suddenly pictures of ponies flooded our group chat. I was still trying to figure out what the hell would make them so weirded out by that when I finally yawned, so I plugged in my phone and went to sleep.

My alarm, the sound of a cow mooing—don't ask, the guys constantly changed it without my knowledge, and I kinda got used to the crazy—went off. I begrudgingly went into the bathroom, brushed my teeth, got as presentable as possible—which actually wasn't all that presentable considering my red hair was basically like a homing beacon for people's eyes. I threw on a pair of clean joggers and a T-shirt, fully prepared to have to deal with the side of Piper that gave me hives.

Paperwork Piper.

Huh, maybe I should start calling her that just to get a reaction out of her. God, I wanted to hide those heels and black pantsuits more than anything. I mean really, who owned that much black? I was a rock star, and even I didn't wear that much black—and it was basically the only friggin' color that didn't clash with my hair!

When I made it into the living room, I nearly dropped my phone on the floor. Piper was wearing black jeans and a black T-shirt, but miracles did happen, because she had on black Nikes.

I nearly wept.

When she bent over to organize something, I got the perfect view of an ass that had all my attention and then some. She moved slightly to the right of my gorgeous dining room table, and that's when the bomb went off in my head.

It was like she went to bed thinking, *hmmm this isn't working, maybe he's right,* then woke up and thought, *huzzah, I know what will do the trick, crayons!*

"What. The. Hell." I gaped. "Are you doing?"

"Oh Good!" She clasped her hands together and looked ready to bounce up and down. "Perfect timing! We're going to go over our exercises, not paperwork, but you will be working with paper!" Holy shit, she seemed too proud of herself. I almost didn't want to burst her bubble.

"This?" I pointed. "This is what you took from our conversation last night?" I shook my head. "I mean, are we finger painting?"

"No. Though we can if you want." She grinned. Where the hell did she get all this pep? It was like a Starbucks Christmas commercial had exploded in her little body over the last twelve hours. She rushed me and then held out her hands. "Okay, so I know this is going to seem elementary, but bear with me, all right?"

I was afraid to nod my head as my feet slowly shuffled toward the section of my house that now looked like Hobby Lobby. "Well, you've got me, I'm at least curious. Are we teaching kids or something that's going to be altruistic and remind me how lucky I am to do what I love?"

Her expression fell a bit. "No. Actually, we're going to do something better. We need a place to start, and a vision of what our finish is going to look like."

Thoughts of ponies suddenly exploded in my brain. No, no, no, no.

I swear the world paused and then went into slow motion as her mouth moved to form the words. "Vision board!"

She even clapped in excitement afterwards.

I blamed the guys for manifesting this in my life, cursing them about a million times before I set down my phone and tried to glare. "I'm not making a friggin' vision board."

"Stop being difficult." She rolled her eyes. "Plus, if you're a good boy, I'll even let you use glitter." She smacked me on the shoulder and then shoved me toward the table. All the while, I felt my balls retreating into my body.

Shit.

Chapter Five

Piper

He looked less than enthused. In fact, he looked ready to set fire to the glitter section of the table, and I had worked really hard to make everything look fun. After our talk last night, I'd realized two things. One, he was being open with me, which was good. And two, the professional me, the one who had very serious boundaries in place, wasn't gonna get the job done. So I figured if I stopped being so clinical and opened up a bit, he would respond better.

"How is this supposed to help me?" He crossed his arms, making it impossible for me not to take notice of the lean muscles that bulged. It's like the minute I turned off Life Coach Piper, the girl who found the rock star attractive charged to the surface with a giant roar.

I licked my lips and tried to focus on explaining why this was going to be helpful, but I seemed unable to form words.

He was pretty.

Really pretty.

Focus, Piper!

Still professional. Remember?

I mean, so what if my boyfriend dumped me right before I boarded a plane for Portland, only to be told that the flight was full, and I'd been moved to a middle seat?

It had been a direct flight from LA.

Three hours with no armrest.

But I knew that this was a fresh start, compliments of my ever-changing vision board.

I grinned triumphantly. "Close your eyes."

He stared me down, his blue eyes twinkling with total judgment before he let out a sigh and did as I asked. "You're right, Piper, closing my eyes and pretending nobody can see me is super helpful. Gee, why didn't I think of that? On stage? In front of thousands of people—"

"Sarcasm is oftentimes used as a defense mechanism," I interrupted. "Now keep your eyes closed. Where do you see yourself in one year?"

"Touring," he said quickly. "Hopefully."

"Uh-huh. And where do you see yourself in three years?"

He hesitated for a few seconds. "Making music."

"Five years?"

He sighed heavily. "I don't know, hopefully still doing what I love."

"All right, open your eyes."

He did as instructed. This time his eyes darted down to stare at his bare feet before locking onto mine. "That just proves that music is my life."

"Music can't be your life, Braden." I said it softly, hoping to lessen the blow, but I saw his body flinch as if I'd just shoved him toward a cliff. I grabbed a blank piece of paper and held it out to him. "You can say that music is your life, that you want to do nothing but make music for an eternity. But a human needs more than just something they're passionate about. Wanna know why?"

He sighed and took the empty sheet of paper from my outstretched hand. "Fine, I'll bite. Why?"

"Because you lose who you are when you lose the only thing that gives you purpose. If I took music away from you right now, what exactly would you have, Braden?"

He paled significantly, his bravado almost gone as he shook his head. "I'm not going to let that happen."

I reached out to comfort him. I touched his shoulder, realized how massive it felt beneath my hand, how warm, how right, and shuddered. "I'm not going to let that happen either. That's why I'm here. To help you find your focus, your identity, your purpose so that music isn't just your passion, but also trickles into every area of your life. You aren't just Braden Connor—rock god. You're so much more. And until you see that, see your worth, make a plan..." I grabbed a bottle of the green glitter. "Create a vision where you're not standing still, panicked, in a vicious cycle of fear—"

"I'm not afraid," he snapped.

I tilted my head. "I'm not the one who said it, Braden."

He tensed beneath my hand. And then he reached out and grabbed another glitter container from the table, gave me an annoyed look, and grumbled, "I wanna use the blue." He eyed me up and down. "You know, to match my balls."

I squeezed his shoulder and laughed. "That's the spirit—ish." I didn't ask him why he had blue balls. I didn't even want to go there, even though my curiosity made me want to comment. I put the professional boundary back in place and waited for him to get started.

He exhaled, and then his grin slowly lit up the room. "If I'm playing with glitter, we're going to need alcohol. Take a picture of this and post it to social media, and I'll drive your rental into the ocean. Got it?"

"Got it." I laughed. I didn't have a rental. He was my ride. He was my everything for the coming days, he just didn't know it yet. "Let's get started on that vision board!"

I almost cheered when he pulled out a chair and started organizing all the different pictures and arts and crafts around him, and then his eyes fell to the polaroid camera.

Braden's head lifted. "You up for an adventure, Coach?"

Chapter Six

Piper

I was used to clients just doing what they were told, then finding a breakthrough and moving on. But with Braden, it was like he wanted me to be a part of it, in a big way. So when he said he had an idea, I thought, *oh cool, he's gonna take some pictures of his guitar or something.*

I didn't expect that I'd be gallivanting all over his beachfront property while he took pictures of things he wanted to put on his board.

"It's serene." Braden snapped a picture of the ocean. "No matter what happens in my life, I want the ocean to be something I come back to, something that represents my music and the way I want to inspire the world around me."

I gulped. "That's beautiful."

"You're beautiful." He winked.

I just rolled my eyes. "Flirting with your coach gets you an F."

He cackled out a dark laugh. "Are you saying you want to F me?"

"Ah, middle-school humor, how refreshing," I countered, even though my entire body broke out in chills with the way he was looking at me.

Bad, it was so bad. And totally against the rules of client and coach. But damn, he was impossible *not* to like. Not helpful at the moment when I was starving for more and more of his smiles.

"Admit it, you just won't laugh because you don't want to encourage my very obvious advances."

I frowned. "Obvious advances, huh? You're a flirt. Trust me, I work with guys like you all the time." Lies. I'd never worked with anyone who had Braden's magnetism. It was intimidating and impossible to ignore.

He snapped another picture, this time of my face. "So you work with musically gifted savants who have red hair, mad kissing skills, and big hands? Crazy, and here I thought I was the only one." He winked.

I opened my mouth to say something when he suddenly held out his hands. "Right there, don't move." He lifted the camera and took another shot. His blue eyes were intense, locked onto me so vividly that I forgot to breathe, forgot what I was even there for. Because all I kept thinking about was him. I was here for him, in so many ways.

I'd never been the type of person to make it personal—my job. But with him, it felt that way, and I couldn't figure out why.

On the outside, I was a professional doing her job.

On the inside, I was counting his smiles.

And wondering what I had to sacrifice to get more.

I was greedy for them.

A few days in and the way he looked at me gave me hope that not all guys were narcissistic jerks.

"One more." He smirked. "Jump in the air. I want to take a picture of pure joy."

I burst out laughing. "What makes you think jumping would make me joyful?"

"Oh, you know, just thinking that a life coach very much likes to live for the tiny moments because it reminds her that she's alive."

I gaped. "That was deep."

"Musician." He pointed at himself. "Now jump."

It felt like a double entendre. The air felt pregnant with tension and unspoken meaning. I didn't want to dissect what was happening, so I just listened rather than gave orders.

"Like this?" I jumped into the air, throwing sand while he snapped the picture.

He bent over laughing, and then his eyes got wide.

"What?"

"STOP!" He held out his hands. "Just...don't move!"

I heard "don't move," but the ocean was so loud that I didn't stop moving until I took another step, directly onto something slimy.

"Ew, gross—oh, shit!" I yelped and then went crashing down next to a jellyfish that, even though it looked dead, could still sting the crap out of my foot.

"Piper!" Braden was at my side in an instant. "Thank God it only got the side."

Fire raged over my foot then headed up my ankle and kept going. Tears stung the backs of my eyes and then dropped down my wind-stung cheeks as I whimpered in pain. "Are you sure? Because it feels like it got my entire leg!"

He swiped his thumbs under my eyes, wiping my tears away. "I'm sorry, I should have thought it through. It's jellyfish season. There's more on the beach than usual."

I sniffled as the wind picked up, matting my hair to my tear-stained cheeks, and messing up my lip gloss.

"Up you go." He gently picked me up, cradling me in his arms.

"Oh." I pressed a hand to his chest and watched him steel his expression as he glanced at my foot and started to walk. "You really don't have to—"

"This is my fault." I could feel him limping on his bad leg and hated that I was probably adding to his pain, along with his memory of the incident.

"Brad—"

He shot me a glare. "Let me carry you, Piper."

"Okay." Part of me wondered if he was carrying me out of the guilt that still clung to his memory or if he was just worried.

My ex would have probably asked if he needed to pee on me *Friends* style and then would have documented it for his IG stories because, you know, influencers gotta document it all!

I winced.

"You hanging in there?" Braden asked.

I nodded and then ducked my head against his chest as more tears fell of their own accord.

It was painful, like really painful.

"If that jellyfish wasn't already dead, I'd kill it dead," I said through my teeth as I tried to blink away the hot tears. "Stupid stingers."

Braden smiled down at me as we finally made it back to the boardwalk and then to his massive beach house. "I'm sure you would have put up a killer fight, small-fry."

"Hey!" I sniffled as the burning sensation pulsed around my foot. "I would have."

"Methinks you would have most likely slipped on your ass after trying to throw your shoe at it."

I glared, thankful for the distraction.

He chuckled and then opened the front door and walked me into the living room, setting me on the leather couch and flipping on the fireplace.

Before I knew it, I had a cup full of hot chocolate with a shot of whiskey, and a blanket tucked around my body. Where had he gotten the caretaker skills?

Most guys would be panicking or at the ER.

He walked back into the room his cell pressed to his ear. "Cool, thanks, just drop off the script when you can."

My foot was still throbbing when Braden came over to the couch and sat on the coffee table. "Good news or bad news?"

"I think this is the bad news." I pointed at my elevated foot. It had one angry slash across the left part of it and was still hurting, though I wasn't swelling that much.

Braden let out a chuckle. "All right, good news then. I don't have to whip out any boy parts."

"Huh?" I frowned.

"*Friends!*" He threw his hands up into the air. "And I'd pee on any one of you!" he said in a perfect Joey voice, making me laugh. He winked. "The bad news is that I have to pull out the stinger. I noticed it earlier but wasn't sure if it was best to take you to the ER or not—"

I opened my mouth to say not when he put up his hand, cutting me off.

"Relax. An old friend from high school works at the local hospital as an ER physician. I called him up, and he said as long as you don't have an allergic reaction, and we soak your foot in vinegar and remove the stinger, you'll be good. Though in some pain for the next twenty-four hours, which"—he took a deep breath and winked—"brings me to the good news." Part of his messy red hair fell over his forehead, giving him this beautiful Jamie from *Outlander* look that had my jaw nearly dropping to my waist. Damn, he was so nice to look at. "You get happy drugs!"

He held up his hand for a high five.

I weakly hit it and then sighed. "But what about the vision board?"

He shook his head like he was massively disappointed in me. "I just told you that you get happy drugs, and you're concerned about the vision board?"

"You." I pouted. "I'm here to help you, not the other way around."

He stood and took the mug from my hand, smiling. "We all need help at some point. You help me, I help you."

I sighed. "Does that mean you'll work on the vision board while I sit here with a throbbing foot?"

His blue eyes narrowed. "That depends, will it distract you from the pain until the pills get here?"

I didn't tell him that I wouldn't take the pills anyways, especially when my ex was the sort of guy who stole my painkillers when I had mouth surgery.

It just made me uncomfortable having them anywhere near me now, even though he was out of the picture. I hated what they reminded me of.

"Yes." I finally said. "Watching you work with glitter will most definitely distract me from the throbbing pain in my foot."

He let out a dramatic sigh and went to work grabbing a bowl from the kitchen. Within minutes, he brought it over. It smelled like vinegar, and I made a face as he slowly set it in front of the couch and then went over to my foot to examine it. "One stinger, from what I can tell."

I gulped, suddenly feeling weak. "Thanks, Doc."

He grinned and then pinched me hard on my thigh as he knelt down and pulled the stinger from my foot. "Done." He stopped pinching.

I rubbed my soon-to-be bruised thigh. "What was that for?"

"Didn't want you to feel the stinger removal." He gave me a lazy smile. "I'm a professional, after all."

I gulped when his eyes moved to my mouth. "You feeling any...pain anywhere else?"

Here. I wanted to point to my mouth. I wanted to indicate a few other places as well as a shiver ran down my spine. "N-no."

"Pity." His voice was low, raspy. My body reacted in a very violent way. I told my heart to stop pounding and my brain to stop thinking of him as available.

I sat up as he gently put my foot in the vinegar water, and then he eyed the table with trepidation. Finally, with a sigh, he walked over to the table and picked up a few of the Polaroids he'd taken at the beach. He also grabbed a glue stick and the blue glitter. "I can't believe I'm actually doing this."

I smirked. "It's going to be freeing, just wait."

"Yes, that's exactly what went through my mind when I picked up the exact brand of glue stick I used to lick when I was five—how fucking freeing this is."

"Ah, it all makes sense now. You ate glue when your brain was still underdeveloped. I'm amazed you can tie your shoes."

He flipped me off with a laugh and then said, "You've only seen me in sandals, I could have a shit ton of Velcro sneakers in my closet."

I made a face. "No, that takes away the entire sex appeal thing, doesn't it?"

His head swiveled back in my direction. "I'll be damned! Did you just call me sexy?"

"No." My eyes widened while my body betrayed me by pumping blood into all the wrong areas, including my face, which felt as hot as the sun. "I just meant, you know, to other people, Velcro shoes may kill the sex appeal you have to...others..." I gulped. "Humans." Another gulp and a weak nod.

Braden threw back his head and laughed. "It's okay, I can keep a secret, Piper."

I put my hands over my face and groaned. "Braden, this is my job, be serious."

"Oh." He jerked off the cap to the glue stick and then blew across it. "I'm very, very serious." And then he leaned over until his lips were next to my ear. I could smell the spicy cologne on his skin and nearly felt his pulse. "By the way, I think you're sexy too, in an uptight, wanna-save-the-world sort of way."

"Thank you, I think?" I frowned.

He patted me on the head. "Welcome. Now, stop distracting me. I have a vision to create!"

Chapter Seven

Braden

If I had to do art for a living, I would starve. That was my first thought as the tube of glitter spilled across my board and spread onto my coffee table.

The second thought?

Piper was ridiculously distracting when she wasn't busy being so damn professional.

She watched my every move, and like an idiot, I wanted to impress her with my skills, not my lack of creativity. But it felt like I was back in school waiting for my teacher to either pass or fail me.

I held in my groan. Shit, I would have failed every class if that woman was my teacher, standing there all prim and proper with a black pencil skirt that she'd hike up the minute I grabbed her by the ass and set her on my desk, spreading her legs wide enough to—

"Braden? Are you even listening?"

"Yes," I lied and then met Piper's gorgeous blue eyes. "I was planning…in my head."

"And this, *this* is what you were planning?" She pointed to the board. I'd tried to make a music note out of glue and then attempted to dump the glitter onto the board in an effort to up the cool factor.

Spoiler alert, the music note looked like a dick, and not a nice one. A small, sad dick that would never see any action. Ever.

I tilted my head.

She frowned. "Is that a—?"

"Note," I interrupted. "The glue just didn't stick right…"

"Stick," she repeated and then covered her mouth to stifle a laugh.

I shot her a glare. "Are you making fun of my music note?"

"Are we really calling it that?"

"I'm not drawing random glitter dicks on my vision board!" I huffed. "The glue wasn't sticky!"

"Poor guy." She burst out laughing, and then I was on her. Well, not on her foot, but on her, tickling her sides as she laughed harder.

"Take it back!" I roared, "or I'm going to torture you even more." Hell, I was the one being tortured as she moved beneath me.

This was either a horrible idea or the best I'd ever had.

She sobered at about the same time I stopped tickling her and moved my hands to her face, tilting her chin with my finger. "I like your laugh."

Her eyes darted to my mouth. "Thanks."

I was probably going to get kneed in the balls, but I couldn't let this moment pass. I was sick and tired of moments passing, of not taking opportunities when they presented themselves. If the incident had taught me anything, it was that life's short, so when a beautiful woman is smiling at you and staring at your mouth, you kiss the hell out of her and capture the moment. Because who knows if you'll ever be given the opportunity again?

I leaned down, maybe an inch from her gorgeous, full mouth, only to hear the sound of knocking followed by my front door opening.

I brushed a soft kiss across her lips and whispered, "Damn shame." And then I was up and ready to kill whoever had decided to invite themselves over.

I should have known it would be Zane, followed by Drew.

"Is that a glitter dick?" Zane asked, pointing at the vision board behind me—or lack of one since all I'd managed to do was glue a picture of the beach to the poster board along with a shot of my old guitar and a blue glitter note that looked like a penis.

"No, man," Drew answered for me. "It's a misshapen drumstick."

"Is there a reason you're both here?" I wondered out loud. "Don't you have wives to annoy? Music to write? Birds to chase?"

"That was one time, and Drew was high," Zane pointed out and then shot a look to Piper. "Don't worry, he's on the train now."

"Thanks, man." Drew rolled his eyes. "Anyways, I know you asked Ty to grab the script, probably because he's the least annoying out of all of us—"

"Speak for yourself," Zane interrupted, pulling a marshmallow out of his pocket and shoving it into his mouth.

I think it was the pregnant pause of silence that followed that had him flipping us all off.

"Anyways," Drew said slowly. "Apparently date night was starting earlier than he thought, so he gave us the difficult task of walking into Safeway without getting mobbed. We wore disguises. You're welcome."

He tossed me the white bag full of pain pills and then smiled down at Piper. "Be honest, did he pee on you?"

She rolled her eyes. "No, he didn't have to. But it did hurt like hell."

"Hmmm." Zane piped up. "Curious minds would like to know why you were out in the sand with Braden in the first place. You know he's terrified of water, right?"

"Huh?" Piper shot me a look.

I just shook my head at Zane. "Correction, my mom's afraid of water and didn't want me going too far out into the ocean. So she told me we had killer squid on the Oregon coast to keep me from swimming. It worked, by the way. Haven't gone in past my waist in years."

"So sad, man." Drew laughed. "You need therapy."

He said it jokingly, but it felt like he'd just exposed the giant elephant in the room. Because duh, I'd been in therapy for months, that's why Piper was here.

Last resort.

And I'd just kissed her.

Hit on her.

Great.

Please let her be cool about the fact that I genuinely liked her enough to explore more kissing, fewer clothes, bared skin.

"He's an ass." Zane finally said and then went over to the coffee table. "So why the art project? It almost looks like you're making a—" He stopped, looked at Piper, then at me. "Please, God, tell me you're forcing him to make a vision board."

Piper grinned. "For the next two weeks, he has to add one new object or dream."

"Isn't that special?" Zane gave me a cheeky grin. "You know, I have a vision board at home. Wife won't go near it because of the pony, but whatever."

"Pony?" Piper asked.

"Nope." Drew moved his hands. "It's creepy as hell, and I'm still not over it, man. None of us are. Anyways,"—he jerked his head toward the door—"we should be going so you can get back to your...glitter penis."

I growled. "It's a music note!"

Zane and Drew walked around the poster board as if they were inspecting it and then looked up at me.

Zane was the first to speak. "I'm actually shocked you're a musician, man. Gotta be honest, that's some shit work. You should really apply yourself to this whole thing, you know?"

I clenched my fists. "Out."

"What?" Zane shrugged.

Drew shoved him toward the door and called back over his shoulder, "Don't kill him, Piper. I want him for the tour!"

"I'll let you know when I get tempted. Not *if*," she called back.

"See? I like her!" Drew answered, and then the door clicked shut.

I opened the white paper bag. "Sorry my friends are idiots. All right, so it says you should take one to two every four hours."

"Actually"—she licked her lips and suddenly paled—"I'm feeling a lot better right now."

I frowned. "Less than an hour ago, you were crying. I'm not buying it."

Her eyes seemed to fill with more unshed tears as she looked down at the blanket. "I um, I just don't like pills."

"Because you like being in pain?" I asked, trying to understand.

"No." She gulped. "Look, it's not a big deal. I just got out of a really bad relationship, and my ex abused pills a lot. He stole my pain meds last year when I had mouth surgery, and ever since, I just...I look at them and I think about his addiction. The way he always justified it like he could stop at any time. He was a lot of things, but he got a lot worse when it went from a pill here or there to stealing stashes and purchasing them from friends, you know?"

Stunned, I just stared at her. "I know you don't know me or trust me, but I would never do that. You know that, right? The guys and I, we're all clean. We have a no-drug policy. Hell, we don't even smoke pot, and it's legal."

"Yeah, well." She crossed her arms, and that's when I noticed she was shaking.

Shit.

I grabbed the pills and sat down next to her, then put a hand on her thigh. "I know a little about trauma." Shit, was I really going there?

Apparently. "I also know that if you ignore it, it just gets worse. I mean, look at me. I literally ran off stage and took the first flight out because of supposed stage fright, when we all know the real reason I bailed. The real reason I couldn't keep singing."

The room fell silent.

She reached for my hand and squeezed it. "You don't have to tell me, you know."

"I know, which almost makes me want to tell you." I squeezed my eyes shut. "The thing about trauma is that, during it, you're just trying to survive. After, you have so much adrenaline pumping through your system that you don't even realize you're injured mentally or physically. And then when you start to heal, that's when the real pain starts. It's during the healing that you realize you aren't okay. I will one hundred percent go dump these in the toilet if it makes you feel uncomfortable, but I also don't think you should be afraid of something that's supposed to make you feel better. When we're sick, we take medicine, right? I don't want you sitting here in pain all night when you could get some sleep and start to heal."

"I get it. I know how ridiculous it sounds. I just... I think about swallowing a pill and then I think about him getting high," she admitted.

"Well, then maybe you don't swallow," I offered and then smirked. "I meant the pill, by the way."

She burst out laughing and squeezed my hand. "What did you have in mind?"

I shook my head and stared into her eyes. "You don't want to know all the things on my mind right now."

Her tongue peeked out to lick her lower lip. I wanted to capture that mouth and force it to surrender to my kiss.

Instead, I said, "I'll crush up the pill and put it in peanut butter. That way you're eating it, not just swallowing something bitter. You're getting something nourishing, all right?"

She gave me a wary stare. "Maybe."

I opened up the container and dumped the pills onto the table then counted them out loud. I reached for one of the craft markers and wrote on the outside the number fifteen.

"All right, I'm taking this one right here." I held it up. "And since the kitchen is right there, you can watch my amazing doctor skills as I chef up this bad boy. Every time you take one, use the marker, take back that control. All right?"

I handed her the marker and stood.

We didn't talk as I crushed her pill and added it to some peanut butter.

When I walked back over to the couch and sat, she looked up at me with moisture in her eyes. "If I take this, I want something in return."

"Hmmm...wasn't aware we were still negotiating."

Her bright smile was going to inspire a ballad someday, I just knew it. "One trigger. Tell me one trigger on stage relating to the incident."

"Oh, so something easy," I joked.

She put her hand on mine and squeezed, so I spoke. "The people. The biggest trigger is the people. All the excited faces, paying to listen to me sing, paying for a good time. And then I see all the faces that aren't with us anymore, all the people I failed because I didn't provide a safe place for them. So, you see..." I handed her the spoonful of peanut butter. "That's why I'm a little bit hopeless, even for you. They want me on tour, the record company wants me on tour, but a tour means people, and I can't perform knowing I could let them down again. I can't sing about love saving a soul when the very song inspired hatred. I just can't. All it took was a light falling and a superfan waiting for me to mess me up again."

She put the spoon into her mouth and took the peanut-buttered pill then said, "Sure you can. Just like I ate instead of swallowed. We need to find a way to look at those faces in the crowd and use it as inspiration, not see it as failure."

I gulped. "I wish I knew how."

"That's why you have me," she said softly.

I looked up into her blue eyes and sighed. "Promise?"

She nodded her head. "Promise."

Chapter Eight

Piper

He was right.

After about twenty minutes, the pill performed its magic, and I started to feel a little bit better.

Braden continued attempting his glitter music notes, and then he made us sandwiches for dinner. I didn't even ask, didn't need to; he just did things because he was good. I didn't realize how starved I'd been for a partner until Braden. It was absolutely terrifying, knowing my heart already hurt when I thought about leaving him or him going on tour.

The pill made me doze off for a few hours, and before I knew it, the lights were off, and Braden was sitting next to me on the couch. My feet were in his lap, and he was slowly examining the injured one like a doctor would.

"Am I gonna make it?" I said groggily.

"You're awake." He glanced over at me. "Sorry, I just wanted to make sure that you weren't having a reaction. The sting actually looks a lot better, and your foot hasn't swollen any more."

"Good." I yawned. "What time is it?"

"Time for Netflix without the chill." He winked.

I liked my feet in his lap way too much. "I'm sure you'll survive. Besides, I've never really understood that phrase anyways. I mean, if I'm watching something good on Netflix, I'd be pissed if some guy just shoved his tongue down my throat and decided to get me naked."

Braden gave me a sharp look. "I'd be pissed too. One doesn't shove their tongue anywhere. That's like bulldozing a kiss, and a kiss changes based on the environment."

"I'm the one on drugs, right?"

He smirked. "Seriously. I mean, think about it. If you're having a moment, you don't just go for it, you lean in." He grabbed my hand and held it close to his face as his mouth lowered, his eyes locked on mine. "And you very lightly brush your lips across." He did exactly that, making my entire body erupt with goose bumps.

"O-oh." I gulped.

"Though…" He dropped my hand. "Sometimes there's nothing better than just angry, aggressive kissing. But in this instance, I'd probably just knock all the glitter to the floor, which would be a bitch to clean up later. But I'd be so in the moment, I wouldn't care. I'd grip you by the ass and push you down onto the coffee table so I had the perfect angle."

"For my mouth?" I asked, a bit breathless.

His eyebrows rose, and then he lowered his gaze to my thighs. "For my feast."

I clenched my legs together and nearly let out a moan when he slowly removed my feet from his lap, then got on his hands and knees so we were at eye level before he whispered, "But since you're injured…"

I licked my lips. Was he going to kiss me?

"Since I'm injured," I repeated breathlessly.

He cupped my face with both hands. "I'd be tender. So tender, you'd barely feel my lips brush across yours."

I gulped. He was inches from my face. His eyes darted toward my mouth. My entire body ached for him to close the distance; he was too far away.

I must have leaned in first because he met me halfway. His lips were soft, molding to mine like we were made to fit. I could taste wine on his tongue as it slid across mine, igniting a fire in my soul that I'd never felt from a kiss before. It was like I would never be the same again.

He pulled away. His hooded gaze was so sexy that I wanted to grab him by the shirt and jerk him against me. "I take it back."

"Take what back?" I whispered.

"The whole thing about not being on drugs. I think I just found mine." And then he kissed me again and again until I lost count. Until he was suddenly next to me on the couch. Until we were making out like we were in high school.

I lost all track of time, but at some point, he pulled away with a cheeky grin and whispered, "Netflix and chill, any questions?"

"Not anymore." I grinned back at him.

He slowly got up from the couch. I was so disappointed he wasn't taking things further. While at the same time, I wondered how I was going to find my footing and go back to being his life coach after he'd gotten so deep under my skin by way of kissing like a god.

He grabbed my pills, changed the number on the bottle, crushed up another one, and put it in peanut butter, then handed it to me.

I took it and then grabbed my bottled water to wash everything down. He was staring at me funny.

"What?"

Braden grinned. "I was just wondering if it would be gross or insanely erotic if I lined your lips with blueberry jam, took a nice lick, then sucked off your tongue until you orgasmed by way of peanut butter..."

"You—you—" I sputtered. "I don't even know what to *say* to that."

"You say, 'good idea, Braden, let's do that next time. But for now, my lips are bruised, and even though I know you want to see me naked, I'm injured. So, let me sleep—but stay.'"

I nodded. "Yes."

"Good." He left the room and returned with two pillows and a blanket, then lay down right next to the couch and handed me one of the pillows.

I got as comfortable as I could, and then I dropped my hand toward his head and ran my fingers through his hair. "I like your hair."

He snorted. "It's bright."

"It's yours." I shrugged, earning a genuine smile from him.

"Yeah, you need to stop looking at me like that. I'm trying this new thing called self-control, but you're beautiful, and you taste like heaven, and it makes me wonder what you taste like everywhere. I'm pretty sure the damn coffee table is gonna make me hard whenever I glance at it because all I'm going to picture is devouring you on top of it. Sorry, what was I saying again?" He winked.

I burst out laughing and squeezed his hand tighter. "Thanks for carrying me today."

"We all have moments we need to be carried, Piper," he said softly. "I'd be honored to carry you anywhere."

I fell asleep holding his hand and silently wondering how I would ever eventually let it go.

When I woke up, it was to find Braden on the floor, sprawled out and shirtless, allowing me an incredible six-pack-fueled view. His hands were tucked under his pillow, giving him a devastatingly handsome look with his ruffled hair and inked-up skin.

My rock star.

No. Not mine.

Client. He was my client.

Ugh, even my brain was on board with my heart.

I'd known him for what? Almost a week, and already we were kissing. Already, I was breaking so many rules. And for the first time in years, I didn't care. I was putting myself first instead of my job.

It wasn't like we'd slept together. We just kissed. Okay, so we made out, a lot. And flirted. And yeah, I was tempted to grab my pillow and scream into it. I was so in over my head.

I wanted the fantasy of waking up next to him, of being able to just hang out with him. But I needed to help him—by any means necessary. So today I was going to wake up and attempt to keep from begging him to stay home and kiss me all day. Because as good as it sounded, sometimes a person needed saving, even if it was just from themselves. Braden needed that right now more than my kisses.

He turned to his side, making the blanket fall even farther down to his hips. I leaned a little closer to the sofa's edge and studied this new development. Was he in boxers? Briefs?

I gave my head a good shake. I'd never done this before, crossed the professional line with a client. But with Braden, it was like I wasn't even aware it was happening until it was already over.

I finally did grab my pillow and put it over my face, ready to scream when I heard Braden's low chuckle.

"You freaking out or something? Let me know if I need to make chocolate chip pancakes. They solve everything..." His lazy look gave me shivers.

"You should put on clothes." I finally found my voice.

His eyes narrowed. "But do you really want me to? Because I'm pretty sure you were staring mighty hard for the last three minutes while I pretended to be asleep."

"Ass!" I threw my pillow at him but lost my balance and went tumbling off the couch, landing directly on top of him.

"That's better. Why didn't I think of that?" he whispered, running his hands down my back and clenching my ass. I could feel his erection through the blanket, and I was one hundred percent hating my job at the moment.

Wasn't there a song called *Sexual Healing*? I mean if a song's been made about it, it must be true, right?

I groaned and laid my head on his chest. "I'm pretty sure if my boss knew I was straddling you, I'd be fired."

"And I'm pretty sure if you stopped, I would fire you. So…that leaves us with you, straddling me and giving me my favorite good morning hug."

I squeezed a biceps muscle. "You're impossible."

"Thank you." He kissed the top of my head. "So, what torture do you have in store for me today? More glitter dicks? Another eulogy— that was cold, by the way—or are you finally changing your ways, leaving your uptight pantsuits at home and ready for some fun?"

I yawned. "I'll make you a deal. Participate today, and later, we'll do something fun."

"Fun of the sexual variety, or fun like video games? I'm a guy. You gotta make it pretty black and white because my brain is definitely not thinking about Donkey Kong. Then again…"

I burst out laughing and lifted my head. "I promise it's going to be fun, and it will also be a learning experience. As to the rest of it, play your cards right and you may just get to hold my hand."

"Holy shit, really?" He beamed. "For longer than five seconds? I've waited my whole life for this moment."

"Cute."

"Hey, you're the one offering up the big incentives. I'm just reacting like any normal red-blooded man would." I could have sworn he thrust his hips against me.

I narrowed my eyes.

"What?" he said innocently.

"You moved."

"Prove it." He winked.

"See? Impossible."

"It's why you like me." He grinned. "Now, as much as I'm enjoying the slow torture of feeling your thighs wrapped around my body, I need to get up and make us breakfast."

"Your breakfast cooking skills are quite impressive."

He just shrugged as I slowly peeled myself off his body, angry that I had to do it in the first place.

He moved to a sitting position. "I helped my mom once my dad left. Funny story, the minute I started working with Adrenaline, Dad called to tell me he was proud. And then he asked for a loan." He sighed. "Good guy, my dad. How's that for shit parenting?"

"I hope you told him to go to hell," I added with clenched teeth.

Braden winked. "I like your spunk, Coach."

"Ah, back to that again."

"Maybe I like to provoke you."

"Clearly." I yawned and then stared down at his vision board. "You added another picture?"

"Yup." His chest seemed to pop out. "After you fell asleep snoring and drooling all over the place—"

I threw a pillow at him.

"—I thought of something. I realized that even if I couldn't perform, I really enjoy writing, putting my thoughts on paper. Maybe one day I can compose for film or TV. Or maybe even get crazy and write strictly for other people." He pointed to the cut-out picture of *Frozen*. "That was all I had to work with around here. But you gotta admit, *Let it Go* earned millions in royalties, and it makes people happy."

I bit my lip to keep from smiling too widely. "Yes, I especially like the fact that it's next to the glitter dick."

He gasped. "Did my coach just say 'dick?' And here I thought you were so prim and proper. You're just hiding beneath that calm, cool exterior of professionalism. Hurry up, say it again."

"You're too much in the morning." I shook my head. "Coffee?"

"Yeah, about that," He stood and offered me his hand. "Why don't I Door Dash us some shit? I know a place that has scones that make you orgasm on the spot—consider yourself warned. I know you have plans for us, but there's no rush, and you're probably sore."

"Orgasming scones?" I repeated.

"I'm so glad you fixated on my favorite part." He winked.

I rolled my eyes. "Coffee first, then we can work on the vision board. Remember a picture or inspiration a day. And yes, you have to talk about it. And yes, I'm going to start pushing you more and more. That's how the program works. And it does work, Braden. We'll figure this out."

"What if I don't want to?" he suddenly asked, his eyes lazy as they drank me in. "What if I fail on purpose and hold you hostage?"

"Pretty sure that's also called kidnapping." I yawned again. "And you're going on tour, it's important we get you ready for the crowds. Plus, I have another client set up for next month." I hated myself in that moment, hated saying it out loud, admitting it.

I hated everything.

His face fell. "Right. Client. Because there's a lot of us that need help."

"Braden?" I reached for him. "I didn't mean it like that. I just...this is my job. You know I obviously like you, I thought—"

"Nope," he interrupted and grabbed his phone. I could see his arousal through his black briefs and instantly looked away, guilty. I'd had no business kissing him, flirting with him when I was leaving. But I couldn't help myself; it was too easy with him, too easy to get lost in him. "I don't want you explaining anything, least of all to me. I know it's your job. I'm your job. And I don't want to jeopardize that. Besides, it was just kissing, right?"

I gulped then swallowed the golf ball in my throat. "Right."

He stared at me for a bit longer and then whispered, "You're a shit liar, Coach, but don't worry, I won't tell your boss that you're the best kiss of my life, or that I plan on doing it for the next two weeks. It will be our..." He leaned in and pressed a kiss to my neck. "...little..." He jerked me against his chest, his length pulsing between our bodies. "...secret."

I leaned in to kiss him just as his phone went off. With a grin, he pulled away and said, "Looks like the courier's almost here. Be right back. Try not to fall into the fire or get bitten by anything else while I'm gone. All right, small-fry?"

Ugh, I was in so much trouble.

I grabbed the pillow again. This time, I did scream into it.

Too bad it didn't help. If anything, it just made my blood heat even more at the sight of his six-pack as he brought food and coffee back into the room.

"I'll pay you back," I said quickly when he handed me the tray, only to have him pull it back the minute I said that. "What?"

"I have house rules, and those rules state that if I buy food or drink, you don't pay me back. You say 'thank you' and eat with fervor, understood?"

"Understood." I reached for my coffee once more. Again, he pulled it back. "Now what?"

With a wink, he shrugged. "Just like being my provoking self!"

I shook my head slowly and grabbed the cup then tried to stand. He was there in a heartbeat, helping me to my feet, and then he pulled away.

No lingering stares.

No wondering if he was going to kiss me.

Just…being helpful, almost annoyingly platonic.

Ugh, what was wrong with me? Normal adults didn't just make out all day, did they? Maybe they should.

"So." Braden cleared his throat. "Enough with the secrets. What's on our agenda for today? You know, after I add to my very special board."

"Let me drink some coffee, and then we'll go over our plans for the next few days, all right?"

"Yup." He gave me a salute and then handed me a scone. "It's okay if you scream my name. God knows I'll be moaning yours." That was the last thing he said before grabbing his guitar and walking out to the balcony.

My jaw dropped.

He didn't turn around.

Two could play this game.

I took a big bite and yelled. But instead of Braden, I screamed, "Drew."

He turned around so fast he nearly dropped his guitar. "Oh, it's like that, huh?"

I chewed and then started to laugh, only to have him stalk toward me like the sex god he was. He pulled me against him, which was weird since I was still chewing, and then he turned my head to the side and very slowly licked up my neck. He finished the lick with a soft bite, moaning my name, then followed it up with, "Since you needed a proper demonstration."

I swallowed the last bite of my scone. "Of?"

"What I'm thinking of when I eat my orgasmic scone. It will definitely be a tie between licking you and eating it. Then again, I could eat you too." He left me staring at him slack-jawed and more confused than ever.

Later, when I took my shower, I could still feel his tongue on my neck. My breasts felt heavy. My thighs decided they wanted to wrap around his lean body again and again. I was in *way* over my head.

And I would be leaving in two weeks.

Chapter Nine

Braden

Damn, I was losing my mind.

I woke up thinking, *hey, we should see where this incredible thing between us goes*, only to be totally shut down when I realized that this was temporary. Duh, what did I think? That she'd fall madly in love with me? Possibly stay after the twenty-one days were over? I mean, shit, we were already past the five-day mark!

She was attracted to me, I knew it. I also knew she was nervous about crossing lines. But what if I invited her to do just that? I eyed her again. I wasn't giving up, not now, not ever. When I wanted something, I went for it one hundred percent. And I wanted her.

I hated that she'd gotten distant. So, in pure jackass form, I did the same. Until I teased her again and realized I'd rather have twenty-one days of teasing, laughter, and kissing than nothing at all.

Hadn't the incident reminded me of that?

I shuddered.

I could still feel the texture of her skin on my tongue, and damn, she'd tasted sweet. I zeroed in on the coffee table and told myself to cool the hell down. I took a deep breath and walked outside with my coffee. I needed to literally cool my body so I didn't propose sex instead of life coaching.

"All right." Piper nearly sent me over the edge of the balcony with her sudden appearance. She had on a black sundress with a leather jacket, paired with short black boots that were tied loosely around her swollen foot.

Adorable, but not proper beachwear at all.

I eyed her up and down. "Are we going to a seance?"

She ignored me and pulled out a terrifyingly large—you guessed it, black—purse, then threw it over her shoulder. "We're going to go have some fun, converse in large crowds, and then I have a really cool surprise for you."

My eyes narrowed as I pointed at her. "Yeah, that smile right there is a bit terrifying. It's almost like you're plotting to take over the world but do it in an evil way because you're dressed like you're headed to a funeral."

She rolled her eyes. "Put a shirt on. Let's go!"

I pouted. "But I like my abs."

"Yes, so does everyone else. If you want to get mobbed, by all means."

"Solid point." I grinned. "Hey, does everyone include you, Coach?"

She bit her lip.

"Don't be embarrassed. I'll let you touch a bit more. Nobody has to know…"

"Not tempted." Her cheeks flashed red. "But thanks."

"Yeah you are. Come on, one hand on the ab, one hand squeezing the pec, a million times better than your scone."

"Pretty sure even I don't have the self-control to squeeze a pec and an ab at one time and not change our plans." She grinned. "Shirt. Now."

"So you're saying I tempt you." I winked. "Good." I breezed past her back into the living room, then went to my room and pulled down a black graphic T-shirt and added a black beanie to match.

When I got back to the kitchen, she looked like she wanted to say something but didn't.

"What?" I grinned. "Do I have too much black on?"

She sighed in exasperation. "You're impossible."

"Hey! I just wanted to match." I swung my arm around her shoulders. "Let's do this, Coach."

"Has anyone ever told you that you're annoyingly chipper in the mornings?"

"No," I answered honestly. "Because I don't do random sex, so there's no one to wake up to and annoy."

She stopped walking. "What?"

I frowned. "Are you seriously shocked I don't do random hookups?"

Her lips parted and then closed, and she shot me a considering look. "Maybe?"

"Not all rock stars are manwhores with drug addictions, Piper. When I have sex with a girl it's because I'm committed, not because I'm using my fame to get laid."

"That's..." She shook her head. "Very mature of you."

"I want love," I explained and then smirked. "I think I have my next vision board post."

"Make sure to put it far, far away from the glitter dick." She patted me on the shoulder.

"Noted." I laughed. "All right, you wanna take the Jeep or the R8?"

"Jeep." She didn't even hesitate. I was half in love already. It was a test, always a test with women. Do you want the status or the fun? Not that a sports car isn't fun, but it's the beach, not LA.

"Jeep it is." I grabbed the keys from my garage and opened her door for her, then handed her a scarf. "Before you jump to conclusions, I keep this in here for my mom, not for my harem. It will keep your hair from sticking to your lip gloss. My mama raised me right."

Before I could pull away, Piper grabbed me by the arm and then leaned up to kiss me on the cheek. Our eyes locked. "Thank you."

Damn, I wanted that mouth on mine. "Coach, I'll buy you hoards of scarves if that's the result."

"It's not the scarf, it's the unnecessary explanation. I appreciate it. I'm not very, um, trusting. And we aren't even in a relationship, so thank you."

"Not yet, you mean," I said with a challenging grin.

She smiled. "Many have tried, all have failed."

"Clients?"

"Boys," she corrected.

"Good thing I'm all man," was my response as I helped her into her seat and then walked over to my side.

She had no idea the motivation behind it, but she made me feel something I hadn't felt in quite a few months.

Lucky to be alive.

* * * *

I drove us around Seaside, which was always calming. My mom had taken us there every year for Labor Day weekend, and I remembered walking by the beach house thinking, *one day I'm going to be famous enough to buy that house and fix it up.*

I was able to buy it when I was nineteen.

It helped that Seaside was somehow this hidden vacation spot for celebs and musicians. It did rain, but the thing about Seaside precipitation was that it never took away from the beauty of the white sand beaches or the ocean waves as they crashed onto the shore.

"You're quiet," Piper pointed out as I pulled into downtown and parked on the street.

I shrugged. "I mean this as a total compliment, so don't get that look girls get when they want to chop off your balls and feed them to you—but you're easy to be quiet around. It's not forced or awkward, I can just be alone with my thoughts."

Her face broke out into a gorgeous smile that I wanted to kiss until my mouth hurt, the same way my heart did just to touch her. "Thank you."

I grinned. "Did we just have a moment?"

"And you were doing so good, Rock Star."

"Sorry, Coach." I winked. "So I'm parked downtown. What's this fun we're going to have?"

"Follow me." She held out her hand and then seemed to realize this was work and not a date. But I was quick enough to catch her hand and squeeze it, holding it as she led us along the semi-busy sidewalk.

I never thought holding hands with someone would make me smile like an idiot, but here I was, swinging our arms back and forth thinking, *I'm so fucking glad I'm here right now.*

What a frightening thought.

That's what therapists didn't tell you about depression. That the good days are almost more terrifying than the bad days because you've been given the gift of feeling free for a few hours and are petrified that you're going to lose that happiness. So it's almost like you can't enjoy it.

Depression is sort of self-sabotage at times, and I knew I was my own worst enemy, because the minute I started to enjoy myself, I felt guilty about it.

"Hey!" Piper gripped my hand tighter. "Focus on me, okay?"

I exhaled, not realizing I'd been holding my breath. "Okay."

"So, tell me a small goal you have, something you're going to focus on or accomplish during our little trip of fun."

"Hmm, how about we trade?" I teased. "Small goal for a small goal?"

"Ah, he thinks he can negotiate."

I gave a playful shrug. "Probably because he's so sexy."

"Ha!" Piper burst out laughing.

I put my hand on my chest. "You wound me, fair maiden."

"Oh please," She tugged me a bit harder as we picked up our pace then crossed the street onto the boardwalk. "You know you're sexy. It's practically oozing from your pores."

I frowned. "See, I want to see that as a compliment but then you said oozing and pores, and it kinda killed it for me. I'm sure you understand."

She looked around us. "You really don't notice all the stares we're getting or all the cell phones that keep getting pointed in your direction? I swear one girl looked ready to pass out."

I gripped her hand as she led me down toward the aquarium. "Honestly, I don't notice it anymore, especially when the only girl I want to pass out, or *swoon* if you will, has been holding my hand for exactly four and a half minutes." I winked. "I counted."

"So you were counting during our conversation. I must be boring." She laughed.

"Multi-tasker." I pointed at myself with my free hand. "Just tell me when I'm supposed to stop and *oomph*—" I ran right into her as she stopped in front of the aquarium and gave me a triumphant look. "The aquarium?"

"The aquarium," she repeated. "Come on, let's go, the day's burning!"

I followed her inside. "Yeah, I hate to be the needle that bursts the balloon at a toddler's birthday party, but…I've been coming here since I was like ten. I know the seals by name, not by choice, out of necessity so I don't get splashed."

Piper just smiled her sweet smile and paid the six-dollar fee for both of us to get in and get fish to toss to them. I had no choice but to follow her.

Maybe this was just her idea of fun?

Not that it was boring since she was with me, but still.

I took my cup of raw fish and went to the corner. The seals swam around then flipped over and splashed.

Piper laughed and tossed in some fish, and then she started to speak. "I know you think everything we do is juvenile, but I promise it has a purpose. You see that seal over there? The one lying on the cement sleeping?"

"It would be hard not to see him," I said. "He's ginormous."

"He's sleeping, not eating," she pointed out.

"He's probably full from all the food he already ate." I countered.

"Possibly." She tilted her head. "Who's your favorite seal?"

"Seriously?"

She elbowed me.

"Fine, I like Kona over there. She's a bit smaller than the others—" I stopped talking when what looked like a bus full of teens came barreling into the aquarium, purchasing tickets at record speed and joining us over by the seals.

I immediately started sweating.

The guy at the incident, the one who'd caused it, had been in high school, and suffered from some pretty deep psychological issues. He'd thought I was sending him a message in my music to kill everyone at my concert because I was tired of fame.

It was a song about love.

My chest tightened, and I suddenly couldn't breathe.

"I like Kona," Piper finally said. "I think I agree."

"Right." My eyes darted around, trying to focus on something to anchor me so I didn't freak the hell out.

And then a hand touched my back, slipped around me, and clung. It was Piper's hand.

I instantly relaxed and wrapped a protective arm around her.

"The thing about people and crowds," Piper said as the seals swam in circles, "is when we go through something traumatic, when it's related to lots of people, we always look inward. We imagine everyone's looking at us, judging us. Maybe they're hiding a knife, perhaps they're insane, maybe they're going to charge. The thoughts become so chaotic that all you can focus on is the maybes and the what-ifs."

I exhaled a shaky breath. "Not really helping, Piper."

"But," she continued, "is anyone even looking in your direction?"

I frowned. "Give it time."

"Hey!" she shouted. "Holy shit, is that Braden Connor?"

All attention turned to me.

That was it. I was going to throw her over my shoulder and march out of here then tie her to my bed.

Way better idea.

A few people nodded in my direction, while a couple of girls took pictures. Then one approached, at a safe distance. "Hi, I know you're with your girlfriend, but can we take a selfie?"

It was on the tip of my tongue to tell her no, but then I realized it was because I was petrified of a sixteen-year-old girl with braces.

How's that for a come-to-Jesus moment?

"Sure." I nodded and gave her a warm smile. "I always have time for fans."

"Awesome!" She bounced up on her Converses and then held up her phone. She snapped a few shots while making a peace sign.

Slowly, a few others drifted up until most of them just moved into a different part of the aquarium.

"So," Piper said when they were all but gone, "what's the verdict?"

"You mean before or after you nearly gave me a heart attack and made me want to tie you to my bed as punishment?"

"Really? That would be a punishment? Something I don't know, Braden?"

I let out a little growl, grabbed her by the hand, and pushed her up against the wall of the aquarium. I captured her lip between my teeth before kissing down her neck and then back up, tasting her skin, only to find her mouth again. I parted it with my tongue and wished I was parting something else.

She moaned into my mouth and then threw her arms around my neck. I lifted her up against the wall, pressing her into it, pinning her there with my body as I deepened the kiss, only to pull away and murmur against her ear, "That was a thank-you kiss."

"I liked it." Her chest heaved while her blue eyes searched mine. "It's okay to be afraid, Braden. What's not okay is letting that fear take away what makes your heart beat."

"*You* make my heart beat," I whispered.

She cupped my cheek with her hand. "I was talking about music."

"Can't it beat for both?" I asked.

She nodded, not saying anything, and then kissed me again.

Behind us, a throat cleared, and I broke away from her only to see a few of the high schoolers from before holding up their cell phones with grins on their faces.

I burst out laughing. "Ah, caught red-handed. Thanks, guys."

They all chuckled and then went back to their business while I slowly let Piper go.

I hated every second she wasn't in my arms.

Piper gave me a huge grin and then whispered, "Time for the rest of your surprise."

"You naked?"

"Be serious."

My dick strained against my jeans, reminding me that one of us, at least, *was* serious. "Coach…"

She just sighed like I was impossible, which I was because I was me, and she was her.

"Let's go, Braden."

I held out my hand. "Aren't you forgetting something?"

She took it and smiled. "How could I? It's all I keep thinking about, holding your hand in one hand and trying to calm my racing heart with the other."

"How's that working out for you?"

She placed my hand on her chest and whispered, "What do you think?"

I stayed quiet, allowed my mind to wander as I registered the heavy *thud-thud* of her heart beneath my palm. And then I said, "I think I want it to beat for me more than I want anything else."

Tears filled her eyes as she gave me a small nod.

We walked in silence out of the aquarium and then headed downtown. We covered all of Main Street until we hit one of my favorite restaurants. The Seaside Grill, home of the best fish and chips a person could ask for—and also a really cool place to hang outside with their outdoor patio, heaters, and firepits.

The minute she led me up the stairs, I paused.

The entire band was there.

All of Adrenaline, Ty, Will, Drew, and Trevor. And the guys from AD2 who were also going on tour with us, Demetri and Alec. Finally, Zane. They were without their wives and girlfriends, which was just about as easy as asking for world peace.

I gaped. "Are we having…bro night?"

"Huzzah!" Demetri lifted a cider and then said, "The wives did put forth rules, however."

I laughed. "Let me guess, only chick drinks and bring home fries?"

"Basically," Zane grumbled and crossed his arms, staring at his cider like it was going to attack him.

For the most part, none of the guys drank because it was too easy to make it a crutch on the road, and also because most of them had dealt with a lot of heroin and cocaine addictions over the years. Ergo, they just stayed clear of it entirely. The fact that they were out here with me? Miracle.

Piper let go of my hand and then pulled me in for a hug. "Have fun."

"Wait!" I tugged her back. "Where the hell do you think you're going?"

"No girls allowed." She crossed her arms.

I rolled my eyes. "Well, I'm your ride, and this is my surprise, right?"

She nodded.

"Then you stay." I grinned. "Hope you can handle a bunch of washed-up rock stars."

"Heard that!" Alec shouted.

I always gave them shit, but AD2 had sold millions upon millions of albums. Even in their late twenties, they were still going strong. Adrenaline had just released a second album while Drew had done a solo release, the one I'd headlined for, and sold another ten million. Between them and Zane, it was like rock star royalty at that table, and I was the lucky one who counted all of them as mentors and friends—at least when they weren't being dicks via text message.

"Come on." I walked her toward the table and pulled out her chair.

"Holy shit." Zane grinned from ear to ear. "Did you just grow manners?"

"Bro, yesterday I saw chin hair. He can finally get a beard too. Wild, right?" Ty joined in.

I glared at them both. "I have manners, and stop making it sound like you picked me up off the streets of Portland's homeless section."

Drew shrugged. "I mean, we did save your life. But yeah, sure, downplay it all you want."

I gave him the finger.

Alec and Demetri eyed Piper up and down and then looked at me. I knew the questions were swirling between them.

"What?" I prodded.

Demetri was the first to flash a flirty grin. "So, how's the kissing?"

Piper's eyes went wide. "How'd you know?"

"Yes!" Demetri shot to his feet and held out his hand to Will, who was also my agent. He slapped a hundred-dollar bill into Demetri's hand. "Pleasure doing business with you, William."

"Bite me." Will glared and then gave Piper a soft look. "Don't worry, it's the only thing we bet on."

"Speak for yourself," Drew said from his end of the table. "I saw sparks on day one."

Zane just nodded. "He nearly combusted on the spot. It was cute. God, I hate how fast they grow." He wiped fake tears from under his eyes while I tossed a fork in his direction. The bastard caught it with one hand and winked.

"Be nice." I glared. "All of you."

Trevor reached for his cider and tilted his head like he was trying to figure out how to ask a question. Finally, he just said, "How's it been going?"

Code for: *Are you going to be able to tour?*

I took a deep breath and said, "Well this one over here"—I pointed to Piper—"just announced my name by the seals where a dozen of Seaside High's finest were hanging out with cell phones. I didn't shit myself or puke in the corner, so…I'm doing better. I guess."

"Bro!" Trevor gave me a fist bump while Drew and Zane shared a look with Piper.

"Yeah." I shrugged. "I mean, we're only what? Six days in? Hopefully, it just gets better and better."

"Ask him about the dick on his vision board," Drew blurted.

I glared. "For the last time, it was a music note!"

"Yeah." Zane snorted and made air quotes with his fingers. "A music note."

Piper burst out laughing. "I think the glitter was my favorite part."

"Hold up," Alec held out his hand. "Did you really force him to make a vision board…with glitter?"

"Yup." Piper looked so damn proud, even I was amused. "And he's doing a really good job. You know, when he's not using his powers for evil like gluing glitter dicks."

"And here I thought he was all grown up." Zane sighed and shook his head. "You'll have to be patient with our young Braden. He's clearly still pubescent."

"Please don't force him to pull something out to prove how not pubescent he is. We don't need that shit on the news." Will groaned. Ha, he knew me well, because I'd been tempted.

"Nah." I shot a smile to Piper. "No pulling out parts in front of a lady."

Demetri laughed. "Bro, that's because you'd go to jail."

"He's not wrong," Alex chimed in.

I stole some of their fries and then ordered a cider when the waiter came, only to be shocked as hell when Piper ordered a beer.

The entire table fell silent, but she simply gave us all an innocent look and said, "What? I'm not under the cider rule, so I'm gonna enjoy a nice IPA."

"Why does that sound like dirty talk?" I wondered out loud. "Anyone else feel affected by the word *beer*?"

All hands rose.

Piper grinned. "I think I like you guys."

"We're super likable, just ask our wives," Zane said smoothly, earning a smack in the back of his head by Drew. "What?"

"You literally slept on the couch last night because you wouldn't get your wife ice cream."

"It was *four a.m.*!" Zane argued. "The store wasn't even open, and then she said if I was a good husband, I would *make some*. To which I replied, 'From what? The goat next door?' She straight-up pointed to the door and said, 'Come back with the goat milk or you're sleeping on the couch.'" He shrugged. "I attempted to explain to the neighbor, but the goat's a pet, and then you have to like"—he made a pinching motion with his fingers—"do this weird tug and pull. It felt very uncomfortable watching those YouTube videos, so I came back and took the couch."

"I miss Nat being pregnant," Alec said dreamily. "She had so much junk food in the house, it was heaven. Now we have kale and vegan butter."

I made a face. "What the hell is that made of?"

"Not *food*!" Alec pounded his hand on the table.

"Hear, hear." Will lifted his cider, and everyone cheered. Piper just sat there slack-jawed.

I elbowed her. "You'll get used to them."

Her face fell a bit. I wasn't sure why, but it was like some of the light had left her eyes. I hated that my words made her feel that way.

The rest of the night went by in a blur. We laughed, we ate, we each had one cider, and as instructed, everyone got home at a decent hour.

Us included.

And just like that, we fell back into our nightly routine, moving around the house like we'd lived together for years. I put on my sweats, she put on her sexy sleep set, and we fell asleep in the living room.

Me with a smile on my face, holding her hand.

Her with a smile on her face, holding my heart.

Chapter Ten

Piper

I woke up smiling, a first for me. Braden was still sleeping soundly, so I tiptoed around him to grab my phone and frowned.

My boss had called six times.

Panicked, I quickly dialed the number.

He picked up on the first ring. "Piper."

"Larry." I cleared my throat. "What's going on? Are you okay?"

"Piper, I think you should sit down."

My heart was in my throat as I sat down on one of the bar stools. Braden stretched his arms over his head then shot me a curious look.

I mouthed, "*Boss.*"

He nodded and then started getting up and moving into the kitchen.

"I'm sitting," I said in a weak voice.

"Have you seen the news recently?"

"No." I frowned. "I've been working."

"That's the thing, though. You know how the media can be. Maybe you are working, but the world now has you pinned as Braden Connor's new girlfriend. It's all over social media, as is our company name and speculation that you were sent to help him only to snatch him up yourself."

I gasped. "I would never—"

"There's pictures. Of you two kissing."

I couldn't deny that, not when I'd participated. "Look, I can explain. Just let me finish up with him and—"

"You aren't getting paid to flirt with the client or to kiss him. You've always followed the rules, Piper, and you're damn good at your job. I honestly thought you could handle this. You've worked with A-list celebrities before. Been hit on numerous times. As your boss, I'm disappointed, but as your friend, I can somewhat understand how it would be easy to fall for someone. You're a fixer. When something's broken, you do whatever you can to make it better. That's why you're good. But we can't have our name attached." His loud sigh sounded like static in my ear. "I'm going to have to let you go."

Tears welled in my eyes and then quickly spilled over. "I...I understand."

"I'm sorry, Piper. Like I said, you're damn good, but this is bad for business. And for any future clients. I'll have your assistant pack up your desk. I did convince the CEO to give you a severance package, even though you're being let go, on account of how many clients you've helped. But as of now, you no longer work for LC Corporations."

I almost dropped the phone as tears slid down my cheeks. "Okay, thank you for letting me work for you for so long."

He sighed again like he wanted to say more but then said, "Piper, as a friend who golfs with your dad and has watched you grow from an insecure teen to the woman you are now, it has to be said. I've never seen you look as happy as you do in the pictures circulating around. Maybe, just maybe, getting fired is the gift, not the punishment."

I couldn't speak for a few seconds and then said, "Thank you for saying that."

"Anytime."

"Goodbye."

"Goodbye, Piper."

I hung up the phone and stared at it.

Within seconds, Braden was in front of me, cupping my face and wiping my tears with his thumbs. He didn't ask what was wrong, he didn't even ask what had happened. All he did was pull me into his arms and whisper, "I'm here."

It was exactly what I needed.

I wrapped my arms around him and cried. Cried because it was my own stupid fault, cried because the writing was on the wall. But mainly, I cried because, for the first time in my life, I had no vision. How was I supposed to help Braden if I couldn't even help myself?

After about ten minutes of sniffling against his bare skin, I pulled back and blurted, "I got fired."

"What?" he roared. "How? Why?"

"Pictures of us kissing." I shrugged. "I overstepped. The company can't associate with an employee who basically sets fire to the rules about client and employee relationships."

His face fell. "I pushed you, I pushed this. It's my fault."

I slugged him in the arm. "Trust me, I was very willing."

He pulled me in for a hug. "Please tell me you'll stay anyways."

I sobered. "I don't know, Braden. Technically, I'm not your life coach anymore—"

He put a finger to my lips and whispered, "You're right. Now I'm yours."

Stunned, I could only stare at him, but he just grinned and pulled me to my feet.

"Some really smart, sexy woman once told me to think about what happens when you lose your passion, or maybe even your way." He led me over to the art supplies and pulled out a piece of white poster board. "I think it's about damn time you create a new one. Just promise me I'll be part of it."

I kissed him so hard he fell against the glitter.

He flashed me a wicked grin and then devoured my mouth, pulling back only to say, "Maybe this will be the best thing that's ever happened to you."

"Being jobless and homeless?"

"We'll figure it out. And fun fact, you're sort of kicking back with a guy who's worth like fifty million dollars, give or take a few million when I like to buy a new car. I think you're gonna be just fine."

I frowned. "I can't mooch off you!"

"Sharing. Say it with me, we're sharing. Plus, it looks like you owe me another fifteen days, and I owe you the same. You're not going anywhere, Coach." He brushed a gentle kiss across my lips and whispered, "You're mine."

Chapter Eleven

Braden

I felt so horrible that she got fired that I instantly went into fix-it mode, but I knew I couldn't fix it. And I was part of the reason it'd happened to begin with, so all I could do was support her and help guide her along. In that moment, I realized that was exactly what she'd been doing for me. Guiding me, helping me figure things out. She'd been the rock I needed, the person who pushed me. She didn't judge me, she prodded me regardless of how much I pushed back. So when I suggested she make a new vision board, I figured she'd push like I did.

Instead, she held out her hand and said, "Give me the glitter."

"Roger." I handed it to her and then tossed her the glue stick. "So, what's first?" We had magazines all around us, books, newspaper clippings, crafts, letters. Basically, like a scrapbook store had shit itself on my favorite table. But it was for her, and I didn't care.

She stared down at the board, and then I saw real fear, panic. I quickly squeezed her hand. "Hey, hey, this doesn't mean you can't change your board later. Maybe you just put down something you want to keep doing."

"Helping." She inhaled slowly. "I still want to help people."

"Good. Maybe you write that in glitter to get started, and then we come back to it."

"Okay." She did exactly that, making my board look horrendous in comparison. And then she grabbed a little picture of a puppy that was in a magazine and glued it to the board.

"Um, should I be insulted that you put a puppy on there before my face?"

I was literally on the cover of *Teen Beat* sitting next to her.

"Rock star's got an ego."

"My face is next to your hand!" I pointed out.

She laughed and then eyed the magazine. "Yeah but it's not the best picture of you. I mean, my vision board has to be pretty."

I gasped. "Did you just call me ugly?"

She leveled me with a cool stare as she very slowly walked over to me and picked up a pink marker then straight up drew on my arm. "Sexy."

"I may tattoo that," I whispered. "Since it's technically the only space I have left."

"Ah, so people don't walk up to you and go 'I wonder if he's good-looking or not. Oh thank God he wrote it down!'"

"Hilarious."

"I thought so." She tossed me the marker. "All right, so now what?"

I ran over to the window and looked outside in a panic.

She chased after me. "What? Is there going to be a waterspout?"

I slowly turned. "Do you even know what that is?"

"Yeah, like a water tornado!"

"Do you know where we are?" I said slowly.

She glared. "Why did you run?"

"Oh, that." I smirked. "I was just seeing if pigs were flying. Alas, they're not, so you really did just ask me for direction instead of giving orders." I patted her on the head. "I'm so damn proud."

She swatted my hand away. "Technically, I don't work for you anymore."

"Good." I pushed her against the nearest wall and captured her mouth with mine. "Then you don't have to feel guilty for enjoying this," I murmured against her lips.

She pulled back with a coy smile. "Who says I'm enjoying this?"

I pressed my palm to her chest and found her rapidly beating heart. "This does."

"Maybe I'm just excited about vision boards."

"Maybe you're a little liar," I argued and then slid my hand up her shirt, feeling her bare skin and finding a nipple. I grinned. "Yup, she's a liar."

She let out a little moan, and then I was lifting up her shirt and sucking, swirling my tongue around my new favorite spot and wondering why we hadn't already explored.

Guilt on my part?

Contracts on hers?

Hell, the heart wants what it wants. I'd always heard that from my mom, but I'd never understood it until now. I just wanted her.

Her head fell back, banging against the wall, and a picture crashed to the floor.

We broke apart. I laughed since I'd just been thinking about my mother. "It's okay, it was just a picture of my mom, no big."

"Oh no, really?"

"Yeah maybe just don't mention that to her when you meet her. Like, 'Oh yeah, he was totally sucking off my right tit and then bam, I nearly orgasmed, hit my head against the wall, and your picture just...died.'"

Her face flamed red like a tomato. "That's...I would never!"

"You're beautiful when you're embarrassed and horrified because of me. It's kind of a turn on, you know?"

She shoved playfully at my chest. "All right, so, we have the rest of the day, and you're still not ready to go on tour. What are you ready to do? What's going to get you prepared for the crowds, the noise, the stares?"

I tilted my head and really thought about it. "Maybe the dark?"

"The dark?" she repeated. "Like hiding out in the dark?"

"No. Like going to the movies dark. You can still see things, but you have to focus harder. It was really dark that night." A tremor rippled along my spine until I started to shake a bit.

Warm palms settled against my cheeks as she cupped them gently, and I looked up.

"Sorry."

"Don't apologize," she pleaded softly.

"It's a vicious cycle, you know, re-living that moment."

"The news said you saved a lot of people," she whispered in comfort.

I scowled. "Saved? *Saved?*"

"Braden—"

"Fuck them!" I roared. "It was because of my music that the dickhead was even there. As if I would somehow send a fan a secret message to kill all my other fans! He was psychotic! No, I didn't save shit. Five people still died, at my concert, with my music playing, with me singing on stage. I got fucking shot in the leg. I didn't save shit. I might as well have been holding the damn gun, pulling the fucking trigger myself." I shook my head and stomped away, pissed at myself for blowing up, pissed that I was talking about it, just pissed.

I charged into my room and threw my fist against the wall.

Maybe I wasn't scared.

Perhaps what I thought was fear was anger and rage. Not even directed toward the shooter but at myself because I should have seen. I should have known. I should have acted faster. The music had been too loud. I was too into the dance sequence going on around me, tuned in to the screams of my name, living it up without even knowing that people around me were dying…for one whole minute, I had kept singing.

And then a girl in front of me just…fell, blood all over her. I grabbed her and pulled her up onto the stage, and then kept grabbing people, as many people as I could. I shouted.

Nobody heard.

I slumped against the floor and held my face in my hands.

A knock sounded on the door, and then Piper was walking in my room, sitting down next to me and putting her head on my shoulder like I hadn't just lost my shit all over her. As if it was her fault that I was messed up.

I sighed and then opened my mouth. "She was sixteen."

Piper just listened.

"She had her whole life to look forward to. Had a shirt that said *number one fan.* Later on at the funeral, her parents handed me her poster. It said, *Thank you for changing my life.*" I felt the familiar tears welling in my eyes. "I changed it, all right. She's dead because all she wanted for her sixteenth birthday was to see the great Braden Connor."

Piper squeezed my arm. "Do you think that she was happy that night?"

I jerked my head toward her. "Happy to be shot?"

She gave a quick shake of her head. "Before everything happened. Do you think she was excited to be there? Do you think she wanted to be there? That she was inspired by you?"

"Yeah, I guess."

"Okay then," Piper said. "Braden, the world sucks, bad things happen all the time, and people are crazy. We know this. You didn't write that song or any of your songs with some weird hidden agenda. You wrote them because you couldn't *not* write them."

My throat felt thick. "I have to get the words out. If I don't, I feel like I'll die too."

"It wasn't your fault."

"See, people say that, but those deaths, they're on me. And every time I perform, I just think, *what if it happens again*? I'm so paranoid. I'm stiff on stage, I can't even entertain anymore. I feel broken."

"Maybe that's your answer."

"Quitting?"

"No." She cupped my face with her hands. "Using the brokenness to help everyone else heal along with you."

I gulped. "How do I do that?"

She got up and went over to my bed, then grabbed the yellow notepad and tossed it to me with a pen. "You said you can't *not* write. So write your pain. Write your truth and help the families heal with you. Help your fans heal. Because they need you now, more than ever."

And then she left.

I burst into tears on my bedroom floor, sobs racking my body until every one of my muscles ached, the emptiness that gave my chest the hollow feeling sucking my body in on itself.

I wasn't sure what time it was when I finally stopped crying and started writing, but I did end up finishing a song. With my guitar in one hand, and my notepad in the other, I walked barefoot into the living room, searching for Piper.

She was sitting on the couch, cheating on me by skipping ahead episodes on *The Witcher*. Still, she'd just saved my career, so I figured I'd forgive her just about anything in that moment.

I cleared my throat.

She paused the TV and turned, giving me a sheepish look. "Sorry?"

"No, you're not." I grinned. "Also, I'm the one who's sorry. I didn't mean to freak out. I just...thank you for sticking by me. For coming into my room when I was a grumpy bear ready to destroy everything in my path."

"Tiger," she corrected. "Bears have brown hair."

I smiled at that. "Angry tiger then."

"What's up?" She hugged a pillow.

I was suddenly so nervous I wanted to puke. I cleared my throat and then did it again, then sat down so I could just get it all out. "I wrote a song."

"Good!" She seemed genuinely excited, which gave me more

courage.

"It's kind of…sketchy because it's new, but, *wow,* this feels really difficult for some reason. Would you listen to it?"

Her smile was so huge, I wanted to kiss her. "I want nothing more."

"Okay." The damn throat clearing was going to be the death of me as I sat my notepad down with all its scribbles, grabbed my pick, and started strumming the haunting melody. It was my first song using F-minor, but it worked. I didn't know how the hell it did, but it just did.

I opened my mouth and started to sing. "It isn't easy when you lose it all. When you see the ones you love fall. When destruction does its worst, while you're trying so damn hard to do your best. But the world keeps turning, we keep fighting. In the end, that's how we honor the dying. Forward not backwards, strong not weak, survivors are we, survivors we'll be."

Tears ran down Piper's cheeks as I moved to the chorus.

"I never thought my feet would take me here, and yet all I have is fear. But we keep going, no choice to stay the course. And know the force of love is all we need, just the slow rhythm and beat of the heart inside, of the life we were given when others died. This is our anthem, our new song, repeat it over and over for the gone."

I stopped playing and gazed back into Piper's eyes.

Her beautiful face was streaked with tears, and then she launched herself across the couch, grabbed my face, and kissed me everywhere she could.

I dropped my guitar onto the carpet and kissed her back hard, as much as I could, trying to show her my gratitude. The love I felt budding in my chest, the way she made me feel when she had no reason to stay but did anyway.

I picked her up and set her in my lap.

And then she was pulling at my shirt.

I wondered how I'd ever lived without her hands touching my skin. My shirt went flying, followed by hers, and then I just went for it, unhooking her bra, cupping her perfectly full breasts in my hands. They were so sensitive I could feel every gasp, every moan as I kissed her again, while she went for the button of my jeans and gripped my length in her hand.

I hadn't been lying when I'd said I didn't do one-night stands. I'd had sex in high school then promptly stopped once I started getting famous because I had no idea if it was real or if I was just a celeb they wanted to screw.

So, it had been a few years.

I groaned, feeling myself harden in her hand to a painful degree as my body surged with adrenaline, need, and a greedy desire to bite and mark every inch of her skin.

"Damn, your hand feels good," I muttered against her mouth.

"I bet I know what would feel better," she teased.

And then I did it.

I gripped her by the ass and laid her across my coffee table, jerking off her sweats in the process, leaving her in nothing but a pair of pale pink underwear that I was going to rip off of her with my teeth. Okay ,maybe not. *Be a gentleman, not a caveman.* I pulled them down to her ankles and threw them next to the rest of our clothes. "I'm suddenly so thankful I missed dinner."

"What——?" Her hips bucked off the table as I licked, exploring her like she was mine—because she was, no take backs. Ever. Her soft moans and breathless pants were like little instructions for where she wanted my tongue, where she wanted my hands as they freely roamed up her body. My fingers dug into her thighs, holding her in place as she went wild beneath my mouth. "You taste…" I wanted to roar. "Like dessert." I looked up. "Apologies for calling you dinner." And then I used one finger, then two, and felt the exact spot she needed me the most as her legs shook around me.

The minute my fingers touched, she was gone, and I finally heard what I'd been waiting for all my life—my girl screaming my name as she felt her release.

My girl.

The one made for me.

The one who didn't care that I was broken and kissed me anyway.

I crawled up her body and kissed her, swirling my tongue around hers, tasting her, knowing she tasted herself on me. I got so ridiculously turned on that she did, I almost lost all control.

I gripped her wrists, pinning them over her head. "Tell me you'll stay."

Tears filled her eyes. "I think leaving right now would destroy me."

"I need you," I admitted. "But if you want to stop…"

"I need you too," she confessed. "Have me. I've been yours since the minute you called me out on my missing buttons."

With a laugh, I kissed her again then lowered my body over hers, enjoying the sensation of our skin meeting. It was like writing the perfect song, the way her body played for me. The little sounds she made that told me she was desperate for me and me alone.

Addicting.

I kissed her harder and then teased her entrance, only to have Piper, play-by-the-rules Piper, hook her ankles around me and pull me in all the way to the hilt.

I almost blacked out as sweat pooled at the small of my back. Before my body could take over, my mind caught up, and I froze.

"Uh, Piper…? I don't do one-night stands, but we didn't use any protec—"

She cut me off with a hard kiss and a whispered, "I'm on the pill." And then *she* moved her hips, not me.

I loved it.

I loved that she created her own music with her body and didn't give a damn that I was on top of her, that I was the guy. She knew herself, knew what she wanted. I would be her slave forever and ever if that's what it took.

I angled myself higher and met her movements, gripping her ass with each deep thrust. Her muscles tightened around me as she squeezed; she was going to kill me before the night was over.

And I was okay with that because I suddenly realized that even if I had been spared for this moment, I would be thankful for it. Because I was happy. Just like the people at my concert. Happy. Fulfilled. Full.

I captured her mouth with my lips and pumped harder, pulling a thigh higher over my shoulder before feeling her contract around me and scratch her nails down my arms, her body shuddering beneath me.

Watching her climax was so much better than Netflix.

She opened her eyes.

And then I was gone because her eyes said so much more than her body ever could.

Her eyes said, *"Mine"* right back at me.

I knew my life would never be the same again.

Chapter Twelve

Piper

Had I still been employed, I would have felt so guilty, I likely would have confessed to my boss right away.

But I wasn't.

I let myself relax in Braden's arms. When he carried me to his bed later, both of us completely naked, and refused to let me put on clothes, I smiled so hard my face hurt.

When he brought out chocolate syrup and said he was still hungry, I let him lick it off my body and nearly died from the way his lips tasted afterward.

Like me, him…and *chocolate*.

Minutes later, he was pulling me into his shower, and I was dropping to my knees, taking him into my mouth. I explored him like he had me, loving like he did, and I wondered how I would ever let this guy go.

Why would I ever want to?

But how could it work?

His hands dug into my hair as I teased the tip of him. When I took him in fully, his massive body shuddered, losing all control.

"Your mouth," he hissed. "Damn, you make me high, Piper."

I just grinned and then ate my dessert the same way he had. By the time we made it to bed, it was three a.m., and I was exhausted. Braden tucked me into his body and kissed the top of my head, then whispered, "Thank you."

I wasn't sure if he was thanking me for helping him or for the sex, but I still fell asleep with a smile on my face, only to wake up and find him gone.

I frowned and then stretched my arms overhead and grabbed one of his shirts and a pair of sweats off the floor.

I probably looked like hell, but I didn't care.

"Oh shit." Drew took one look at me and then looked away. Zane sighed and then handed Drew a twenty.

"Really?" My eyes narrowed.

"What?" Zane shrugged. "We get bored in Seaside, and he's perfect for you. So, yeah, we made a tiny bet. By the way, he's out grabbing you breakfast. We were told to make sure you didn't panic when you woke up. Would have helped if he told us more details, but yeah…."

I gulped. "I was fired."

"Son of a bitch!" Drew roared. "I'll call them right now—"

"No, no, no, that's not—it doesn't matter. I'm thankful. We're still working together, and things are good. Actually, I'm glad you're here. I had an idea. Think of it as the final push."

"I'm listening," Zane said.

"He's been writing, healing through the music, using his brokenness to help his fans as well. I think there's one more thing that would help him reach that final level."

"Done," Drew said without even asking what I was talking about. "When do you want to do this?"

I thought about it for a minute. Selfishly I wanted to do it in a week and a half so if he was pissed, my heart wouldn't be broken when he sent me away.

But the other part of me, the one that wanted to help him, knew that we needed to get him out of his head. So I said, "As soon as possible."

"All right, you have my attention. What's the plan?" Drew sat, and I talked.

By the time Braden came back, we had a solid game plan in place that would either set him off or save his career.

Zane and Drew departed after the breakfast burritos, which left me alone with my favorite person in the world.

"So." Braden smirked. "Movie? Lunch? Vision board?"

"Hey, you owe me two more things on your board."

"Come here." He motioned, then drew a heart on his board and put an arrow through it. Then he wrote *love*. He jotted down a few of the lyrics from his new song. "Done."

Tears filled my eyes. "You know you're pretty romantic for a redhead."

"I'm insulted." He put a hand to his chest. "Hair has nothing to do with romance. Everyone knows it's about the six-pack."

I rolled my eyes. "Let it go."

"I'm not Elsa. Sorry, not sorry."

I burst out laughing. "All right, let's go, Romeo. You still have work to do."

"Work?"

"Write." I grinned. "And I'll job search."

He hesitated. "Job search?"

"I can't live here forever," I joked. "I mean, that's crazy. I need a job, I'm sure something will pop up in LA."

His face fell. "Yeah, you're really talented." His smile returned but it was different. "I believe in you."

"Thanks, Braden."

"If I finish another song, can I lick your—?"

I threw a pillow at him.

"Hey! I was going to say hand!"

"Lies," I deadpanned.

"Fine, I was going to say something way more...pink. Aw, you're blushing, how adorable."

"Braden," I warned.

"Fine." He offered a shrug as if to show he didn't care. "But when I finish my song, I get rewarded, right?"

I tilted my head. "You want me to make you a cake?"

"Um, depends. Are you popping out of it naked?"

"Nah, too messy."

"Well damn, there goes that fantasy."

"I'm a crusher of dreams."

"False." He grinned. "You're the starring role in mine."

I didn't know what to say. When I realized I had rolled my lips inward, I forced myself to relax.

He gave me another sly smile. "I get to kiss something. Promise."

"Promise."

"And, Piper?"

"Yeah?"

"It's going to be about you."

"What is?" I said, curiosity piqued.

"My new song."

My jaw dropped. "Braden, you don't have to—"

"I can't help that you inspire me. Now go job search, and I'll write about this sexy girl in a pantsuit."

"Sounds kind of anal."

"Hey, that's an—"

"Out!" I pointed to the door.

His laughter followed him the entire way to his bedroom.

Chapter Thirteen

Braden

I'd never had a partner before, at least not the sort who took care of me the way Piper did. She randomly dropped off a sandwich when I was writing in my room. Minutes later, a Coke Zero was set on my desk. Hours after that, she came in with another snack and asked how I was doing. All I kept thinking, while my heart was panicking, was how did I ask her to stay without making it weird?

I was torn between trying to write music and attempting to figure out ways to make her stay.

It was more than a crush to me.

More than a one-night, or technically, a multiple-orgasm stand.

I just wanted her, but how did you tell a girl you'd only known a little over a week that you wanted her to stay with you?

I sure as hell couldn't ask her to move in unless I played it cool. Like she could stay with me until she found something solid. But then once she did find something solid, she'd leave.

And asking her to be my roommate meant she'd want to pay me, and that just made me want to fight.

And then there was the tour.

I was technically supposed to be on it in less than ten days if things went well.

Which meant no more Piper, no more laughter, no more sandwiches. And damn, the woman made a good sandwich; she always put in extra mustard like she knew it was all I wanted.

I sighed when my text alert went off.

Mom: **You doing okay?**

Me: **If falling for a beautiful girl and plotting world domination is okay, then yes?**

Mom: **You already dominate my world.**

Me: **I'm blushing.**

Mom: **I miss you.**

Me: **I miss you too. I promise I really am doing okay. I just really like this girl, and she may be leaving. I know kidnapping's illegal, but...**

Mom: **Ha. Don't end up on the evening news. And if you like her, you could always just...ask.**

Me: **Ask?**

Mom: **Ask her to stay. Sometimes the simplest way is the best way.**

Me: **Ugh. How did you get so smart?**

Mom: **I'm a mom, it's in the job description. Tell her how you feel. Honest moments are the best ones, the ones you want to keep, the ones that mean the most.**

Me: **I love you so much.**

Mom: **I know.**

Me: **Arrogance becomes you.**

Mom: **Says the guy who flashes his six-pack on a regular basis on stage.**

Me: **It's in the job description.**

Mom: **Cute. Can we facetime later? I want to see this girl.**

Me: **Absolutely. And Mom? I really like her so maybe don't tell her it took me until I was ten to learn how to tie my shoes the right way.**

Mom: **Sorry, that text didn't come through.**

Me: **MOM!**

Mom: **Will you look at the time?**

Me: **MOOOOMMMMMMMMMM**

Mom: **LOVE YOU!**

I stared down at the phone, irritated but smiling, and then wiped my hands down my face as I thought about it more. Could I just tell Piper how I felt? Even though it was so soon?

I groaned and tossed a pillow to the floor. My mom always did say that when I fell, it would be instant and hard. I remember laughing in her face. Not laughing now. No, I was suffering and wondering how

Piper's phone calls were going, and wishing we were both naked.

"Hey!" Piper knocked on my door. "You okay?"

I looked up. "Is that my shirt?"

Her cheeks turned bright red. "Possibly?"

"Damn, it looks better on you."

"It's black." She grinned, and I tossed a pillow in her direction. She dodged it. Suddenly, she was running toward me and jumping on top of me.

I kissed her first—I think.

Her hands found my face, pulling me closer as she hooked her legs around me.

Bliss.

This was what people wrote love songs about.

This was what people fought wars for.

This feeling right here, where her heart seemed to beat my name.

I wanted to tell her I was keeping her. It was on the tip of my tongue, and I opened my mouth—

"I got an interview."

I stilled, eased out a breath, and tried for a façade of nonchalant interest. "Where at?"

She pulled back and smiled. "It's a secret."

I laughed, even though I wanted to immediately do something illegal like lock her in my room. "Ah, well, I bet I have a few ways to get you to confess."

"Mmm, really?" She tugged my shirt over her head and pressed an open-mouthed kiss against my lips. "Still so sure?"

I couldn't think beyond the word *mine*, so I didn't talk at all. I used my actions to show her how I felt, to show her I was owned. That a life coach had waltzed into my world, tipped it upside down—or maybe right side up—and made me realize that I had something to give the world beyond a gimpy leg, my voice, and my life.

I had my songs.

And that's why we needed music. Because sometimes words weren't enough. But pair those words with notes, and you had a masterpiece that moved people to tears, moved them to action, moved individuals in general.

Piper pulled away and tilted her head. "Did you get a lot of writing done?"

I jerked my chin toward my notepad. "Take a look."

She slowly crawled out of my lap—topless, might I add—then grabbed the yellow notepad and started reading.

I'd never been nervous about anyone going over my lyrics before. Not until that moment. Suddenly, she started wiping tears from her cheeks.

Without speaking, she grabbed the notepad and went into the living room. I slowly followed.

She grabbed my vision board and started drawing.

I let her sketch, though I didn't know how she was seeing through her tears to do it.

When she was done, I was stunned into complete silence.

She'd drawn a small globe and then had written my name over it. After that, she drew a sun next to it.

"I knew you would never put this down, but it needs to be on here. Because the minute this album drops, you're going to change the world with your light, and I'm so damn proud to be a part of it, even in a small way." She turned, and I almost lost it, almost told her I loved her. I knew that my love was too soon, but I didn't care.

Instead, she beat me to it by kissing me again and again. I was lost to her and barely had any time to take her to the couch before our clothes went flying and our touches became a hurried mixture of pain and pleasure. When I thrust into her, felt her heat around me, I knew I would never want anyone else.

Ever.

"Stay," I whispered as we moved in sync.

Her eyes were glassy as she answered, "Where else would I go?"

I flipped onto my back, letting her ride me as she pressed me into the couch, her hair draped over her face.

"Away," I barely squeezed out, finding myself getting choked up. "Would you believe me if I told you, you were my soul?"

"Would you believe me if I told you, you owned my heart?"

Neither of us answered.

But our bodies did.

And in that moment, all I kept thinking was, *thank God I was spared.* Even if it was only for a day. It still meant I had her.

Chapter Fourteen

Piper

Five more days in his arms, that's what the universe gave me, and I told myself to be thankful. Technically, my time was up next week. Even though I wasn't still working for the production company, I was trying to help in small ways. Like attempting to get him to finish a full album and making sure he was nourished enough to do so. I even told my old boss not to send someone new, that I was doing this pro bono, that I refused to leave his side.

Braden was funny when he was writing; it was either food or sex or both. I still hadn't told him who my interview was with. I was too terrified that he'd panic or say no.

And I knew his denial would break me, so I kept it to myself. I decided I'd tell him after the surprise.

I just hoped it worked. It was a last-ditch effort to get him to see that the world needed him and his music. I could only hope that he didn't blame me or panic when he saw what we had planned.

That was the other problem. I'd been half hoping that Drew and Zane wouldn't be able to work miracles that fast, but apparently, money talked. When they called me earlier that day and said that Project Free Braden—Zane's idea, not mine—was a go, I was already mourning the loss of the man who'd stolen my heart with his words. Who made me sigh with his touch.

How did people survive knowing this sort of feeling and then suddenly living without it?

"So that was weird," Braden said as he walked into the room

wearing nothing but low-slung dark jeans that showed off his perfect chest and ramped up his wow factor.

I sighed, totally distracted by his ink and hard muscles.

"Hey, eyes up here." He snapped his fingers. "I'm a person, not a piece of meat!"

I just shook my head. "Not what you said this morning when I had you in my mouth. Pretty sure you said something like, 'Suck me like your favorite lollipop, and I'll call you queen.'"

His grin was smug. "Hey, I'm not the best at dirty talk, all right. But that mouth…" His eyes zeroed in, and suddenly, my black sweater dress felt too tight, like I needed to take it off, get some air, and then some Braden.

"Eyes up here." I winked.

"Yeah, that's fair." He crossed his arms over his chest. "Anyways, Zane just called, which he never does. Thought the dude was in prison or something since he didn't send a text, but he wants us all to go out since we only have a few days left."

I swallowed the giant lump in my throat and nodded. "That sounds fun. Did he say where?"

Braden shrugged. "Said he'd text me in a few minutes. They wanna meet now, is that cool?"

"Yep." I didn't tell him I'd already gotten a text hours ago and had done my hair and makeup since I'd literally lived in Braden's sweats for days, helping him focus and get on track with his music. "You better go put on a shirt so girls don't just swoon at your feet though."

He laughed. "I don't think I've been this shirtless in a long time. And someone keeps stealing my sweats so…"

I bit my bottom lip and gave him an innocent look. "They're comfier than my pantsuits."

He gave me a stunned expression. "Does that mean we can burn them and stay naked?"

"Um, no. Because we still have to go outside this house."

He pouted. "That's not actually accurate. We can get groceries delivered, and food ordered like a date night in. Technically, I could keep you here as my prisoner."

"I'd want nothing more," I said honestly.

His face fell like he knew where my thoughts were headed, and then he was walking over to me and pulling me into his arms.

He would be leaving for his tour soon.

And if I ever wanted to see him again, I needed to ace my interview and hope he didn't get pissed.

The future was so uncertain.

But I knew I could count on his kisses.

On his words.

His touch.

The way he protectively held me close and showed me that he was in this even when nothing was said between us. I clung to him so tightly that I started to get hot.

Finally, he pulled away, kissed my forehead, and whispered, "We'll figure it out, all right?"

"I believe you."

He groaned as his phone went off. "That's probably Zane. Let me go put on a shirt real quick."

"Wear that gray beanie I like too!" I shouted after him. I knew what was coming; he didn't.

"On it!" he called back.

Within minutes, we were in his Jeep headed toward downtown. There were a ton of people. Not just a few clusters, more like hundreds, all going in the same direction we were.

"Shit, is there an event going on?" Braden asked.

"It's Seaside, who knows?" I answered. "Just park wherever, we can walk."

"If we can find parking." He laughed and then a car magically pulled out. We pulled in, and I felt like puking. "God provides."

"Ha." I pressed a hand to my stomach as we joined the crowds of people walking toward the beach, in the direction of the circular drive of the Seaside boardwalk where a stage was set up.

It was already starting to get dark.

Butterflies erupted in my stomach as we finally got close enough to see the stage and the name in front of it.

Adrenaline.

AD2.

Zane "Saint" Andrews.

With special guest, Braden Connor.

He stopped walking and dropped my hand, his gaze on the giant stage with its two TV screens.

There were at least a thousand people already cheering, holding glow sticks. The guys were going on in a few minutes.

"You knew," Braden said in a broken voice.

"It was my idea," I confessed.

"The hell?" He pulled away, his eyes searching mine. "Why? Why would you do this to me? You know I'm not ready! This crowd is huge, and I haven't performed since—"

"Since you freaked out on stage. And before that, since you were shot in the leg by a crazed fan. Since the world heard your name and said prayers that you'd recover, since fans swarmed your social media pages with well wishes and kind words. Yes, I know. Not because I'm your life coach or your friend, or the person who wants to keep you forever, but because I'm a fan. A true one. And because I know that what you have inside here"—I tapped his chest—"is something they need to hear. The world is waiting, Braden. So with each step you take toward that stage, own that fear. Own the way it tastes, the way it tries to choke your truth, tries to silence your voice. Get on that stage and sing the loudest you've ever sung." I dug into my purse and pulled out the pictures of the fans who had died. Most of them were from them posting on social media wearing his merchandise. "Most of all, do it for them." I handed him the pictures.

He looked down and swallowed, his eyes filling with tears. "What if I can't?"

"What if you can? You'll never know unless you try."

With a sigh, he turned and started walking toward the stage. As he walked, the crowd parted, and slowly, so slowly, the fans lifted their glow sticks like a salute as he made it through. And then he saw it.

The front of the stage where the pictures of the people who had died were surrounded by candles.

He stopped and stared while the crowd started chanting his name.

He slowly faced each picture, made the sign of a cross over his chest, and then pointed to the sky.

Cheers erupted from the crowd as he took the stairs up to the stage.

Zane was there, handing him his guitar.

I couldn't hear what they said, but it didn't matter, did it? Because Braden Connor was home.

Chapter Fifteen

Braden

My body was shaking. It was impossible to stop or control. I'd freaked out at a smaller concert, and now this—this was double the size, and they were screaming my name.

The rest of the guys were backing me up, which helped.

I searched the crowd for Piper and found her near the back, smiling. I focused on her face, and then I closed my eyes and thought about all of the people affected by the shooting.

Because it hadn't been an incident, had it?

It was a mass shooting.

Caused by music.

But not caused by me.

I didn't control the guy who'd lost his shit. The only thing I had control over was my reaction.

And I'd let it affect me and my music like a disease.

Suddenly it clicked.

I opened my eyes as a sense of peace descended, because hell if I was going to let that bastard win.

I grabbed my pick and threw my guitar strap around my neck, then went up to the microphone.

The entire crowd went silent immediately.

"Hey, guys." I started strumming. "I'm not gonna lie to you. I'm absolutely terrified to be up here right now. I think it's important we talk about our fears, though. I'm afraid because in the back of my head, I wonder if someone else is going to use my music as a way to act on their own personal pain. And it destroys me to think that my words, words of peace and love, could be used for war, for pain, for personal gain... But someone once told me that sometimes you need to use what makes you feel broken to help heal others. So here I am, revealing my insecurities, my scars, and asking you to feel with me. All the pain, all the fear, all the regret, all the what-ifs. Let the overwhelming sensation of being human wash over you, and be here with me in this moment."

I started my new song, the one I had written when Piper bullied me into using my broken pieces. The minute my voice filled the air, Ty started on the drums, slowly building the haunting melody, the rest of the guys quickly caught on with the harmony. Suddenly, we were a band, all of us. Not just us, but also the crowd.

I was shocked when they started singing along and then noticed both screens held the lyrics.

They all had their glow sticks raised, and when I looked at the front row, I saw several people with pictures of the victims on their shirts with titles like *Gabi's mom, Taylor's dad,* aunts, uncles, and then my mom, grinning from ear to ear. I nearly lost it.

The families were here.

They were here.

At my concert.

Walking in bravery while fear tried to choke them.

And they were singing along.

A tear ran down my cheek as I sang the chorus, and then just when I thought things couldn't get more emotional, the screens next to me changed.

They said:

Austin Shooting Tribute Concert. All proceeds go to victims' families. All money matched by performers.

These guys.

My family.

And that girl.

My world.

I ended the song a minute later, dropped to my knees, and felt my friends behind me. Zane held out his hand, and then I was hugging all of them as background music filled the air.

The crowd cheered. I was so emotionally exhausted, I wanted to sleep for a week.

But I'd done it.

I hadn't run.

I had faced my giant head on.

And I smiled in the face of fear.

Maybe that's how we kept going.

Maybe there was no explanation for why bad things happened. But thank God we had good people on this planet to help us get through it. Those who loved us through our pain and told us it was okay to be scared.

When we were done hugging, Zane grabbed the microphone and started singing one of his newest songs. I fell back with the rest of the guys and played my guitar. I'd helped Zane write this song, after all.

It's what I did.

I wrote words.

I performed.

And tonight, I triumphed.

Chapter Sixteen

Piper

We hadn't had a chance to talk after the concert. Everyone headed to Braden's house, including the wives and kids, for the calmest after-party ever. *Paw Patrol* played in the rec room while the main room had *Frozen Two*. Even some of the dads were watching that with rapt fascination.

"Damn, I wish I had written that song," Zane lamented as *Into the Unknown* played. The guys laughed while the kids tried to sing along.

Pizza was delivered, and all seemed well.

Except I had no idea where Braden and I stood.

I was so proud of him, I wanted to cry. His words would impact the world, like I'd said. I just wanted to be a part of the journey.

"Hey." Will walked up. "Nailed the interview."

I gave him a soft smile. "Thank you."

"Wait." Braden suddenly broke free from Alec and Demetri and pinned Will with his stare. "You knew about the interview?"

Crap.

Will gave me an uneasy look and then held up his hands and backed away slowly.

Braden's hurt expression didn't help things.

"Let's go talk?" I offered, grabbing his hand and pulling him out to the balcony. He grabbed a blanket and wrapped it around my shoulders while I exhaled a shaky breath. "You were great tonight."

"I was petrified," he answered. "I'm glad you didn't tell me. I think it would have made it worse, the anticipation of it all. And when I saw the pictures and the families..." He shook his head. "How is it that you've known me for only thirteen days and know exactly what I need when I need it?"

I smirked. "Life coach."

"Bullshit." He jerked his chin in my direction. "Give me the real answer."

I gulped. "Because I recognize your pain like it's mine, and I would do anything in this world to make it better."

He gasped, and then he pulled me into his arms, tugging me by the blanket. "Stay. I'll do anything if you just stay. Damn it, stay." He kissed my forehead. "Stay." Then my cheeks. "Stay." Then my lips as he whispered across them, "Stay."

A tear ran down my cheek. He caught it with his fingers. "Why does staying make you sad?"

"I was afraid you'd be pissed that I pushed you," I admitted. "Afraid you wouldn't want me to stay after all of this when it's the only thing I want."

Our foreheads touched. "Piper, I would have chased you, tackled you to the ground, and begged you like the obsessed, in-love fool I am."

"Love?" Tears welled. "But it's so soon. Are we crazy for—?"

His mouth found mine, but before the kiss truly got going, he pulled away. "Life is short. Love can be given just as quickly as it can be taken. I'm done living in fear. I just want to live by your side."

I hugged him tightly.

After an intense moment, he abruptly released me. "Be right back."

He was gone maybe thirty seconds, but when he came back, it was with his vision board.

I smiled. "You've been busy."

"Very," he admitted. He pointed to a picture. It was of me before I got stung by the jellyfish. I looked so happy. Underneath it, he had put one word: *forever*.

I gasped. "When did you put this on?"

"Days ago," he said. "And I'm keeping it because I'm keeping you, even if I have to make up a fake job for you so I can have you on tour."

I grinned. "You won't have to."

"Huh?" He put the board down on the table. "Explain."

"That's how Will knew I was interviewing with the production company. Will suggested that they have a life coach on tour to help the guys stay focused on their music and goals, and I nailed the interview. They offered me the job during the concert via email. I leave with you--"

He jerked me against him, meeting my mouth with a punishing kiss, and then he tossed me over his shoulder and marched into the house.

"Daddy, Daddy, why does Uncle B have a girl over his shoulder?" one of the kids asked.

Alec muttered a curse and then said, "Headphones!"

His two kids put their hands on their ears only to have Trevor's eldest demand, "Why are they going to bed already? You said we could stay up late!"

"Uncle B's in trouble, that's why," Drew said, not helpfully. "Hey, let's uh, turn up the volume on *Frozen Two*, and play the sing-along game!"

The kids cheered.

The adults all smirked at us.

And then the door to Braden's room closed.

Clothes were thrown in seconds.

Mouths clashed.

And I was his.

Epilogue

Braden

1 Year Later

"How's it going!" I shouted into the microphone amidst the screams. "We're so glad you guys could come out and join us for our second annual benefit concert to prevent violence."

More cheers.

"And a very special thank you to my gorgeous, pregnant wife for helping us coordinate this very personal project. Let's give her a round of applause." I turned to her stage left.

She was glowing, due in a few days, and I'd never seen anything so beautiful.

The wives were all backstage, while the guys and I were preparing for our sets. I knew Piper would be in good hands with all the ladies—they were used to this sort of thing.

After the sold-out world tour, we decided that we needed to do something more, something better. Because when we sang, people listened.

So we made it an annual concert event in Seaside.

We raised money.

And we tried to create change in a world of people who too often said they agreed with you only to push back when it made them uncomfortable or didn't benefit them.

Piper got pregnant nearly two months after the tour started. I had found her puking her guts out and immediately thought she had the flu, only to be overjoyed when we found out that she was carrying my child.

Didn't matter that we'd fallen quickly. After all, trauma forced you to grow up fast, and I'd been a grown-up since my dad left, taking care of my mom and my family for as long as I could remember.

I grinned at the sold-out crowd camped out on the beach and said a prayer of thanks for the very uptight Pollyanna who had stomped into my life and forced me to make a vision board that was still hanging up in my house, glittery blue penis and all.

In order to change, we sometimes had to get uncomfortable. But it only lasted a minute before you found yourself stepping out of the darkness and into the light.

"Let's get this party started!" I yelled as I strummed the chords to my newest hit single, *Vision.*

* * * *

Also from 1001 Dark Nights and Rachel Van Dyken, discover Abandon, All Stars Fall, and Envy.

Sign up for the 1001 Dark Nights Newsletter
and be entered to win a Tiffany Key necklace.

There's a contest every month!

Go to www.1001DarkNights.com to subscribe.

**As a bonus, all subscribers can download
FIVE FREE exclusive books!**

Discover 1001 Dark Nights Collection Seven

For more information, go to www.1001DarkNights.com.

THE BISHOP by Skye Warren
A Tanglewood Novella

TAKEN WITH YOU by Carrie Ann Ryan
A Fractured Connections Novella

DRAGON LOST by Donna Grant
A Dark Kings Novella

SEXY LOVE by Carly Phillips
A Sexy Series Novella

PROVOKE by Rachel Van Dyken
A Seaside Pictures Novella

RAFE by Sawyer Bennett
An Arizona Vengeance Novella

THE NAUGHTY PRINCESS by Claire Contreras
A Sexy Royals Novella

THE GRAVEYARD SHIFT by Darynda Jones
A Charley Davidson Novella

CHARMED by Lexi Blake
A Masters and Mercenaries Novella

SACRIFICE OF DARKNESS by Alexandra Ivy
A Guardians of Eternity Novella

THE QUEEN by Jen Armentrout
A Wicked Novella

BEGIN AGAIN by Jennifer Probst
A Stay Novella

VIXEN by Rebecca Zanetti
A Dark Protectors/Rebels Novella

SLASH by Laurelin Paige
A Slay Series Novella

THE DEAD HEAT OF SUMMER by Heather Graham
A Krewe of Hunters Novella

WILD FIRE by Kristen Ashley
A Chaos Novella

MORE THAN PROTECT YOU by Shayla Black
A More Than Words Novella

LOVE SONG by Kylie Scott
A Stage Dive Novella

CHERISH ME by J. Kenner
A Stark Ever After Novella

SHINE WITH ME by Kristen Proby
A With Me in Seattle Novella

And new from Blue Box Press:

TEASE ME by J. Kenner
A Stark International Novel

Discover More Rachel Van Dyken

Abandon: A Seaside Pictures Novella
By Rachel Van Dyken

It's not every day you're slapped on stage by two different women you've been dating for the last year.

I know what you're thinking. What sort of ballsy woman gets on stage and slaps a rockstar? Does nobody have self-control anymore? It may have been the talk of the Grammys.

Oh, yeah, forgot to mention that. I, Ty Cuban, was taken down by two psychotic women in front of the entire world. Lucky for us the audience thought it was part of the breakup song my band and I had just finished performing. I was thirty-three, hardly ready to settle down.

Except now it's getting forced on me. Seaside, Oregon. My bandmates were more than happy to settle down, dig their roots into the sand, and start popping out kids. Meanwhile I was still enjoying life.

Until now. Until my forced hiatus teaching freaking guitar lessons at the local studio for the next two months. Part of my punishment, do something for the community while I think deep thoughts about all my life choices.

Sixty days of hell.

It doesn't help that the other volunteer is a past flame that literally looks at me as if I've sold my soul to the devil. She has the voice of an angel and looks to kill—I would know, because she looks ready to kill me every second of every day. I broke her heart when we were on tour together a decade ago.

I'm ready to put the past behind us. She's ready to run me over with her car then stand on top of it and strum her guitar with glee.

Sixty days. I can do anything for sixty days. Including making the sexy Von Abigail fall for me all over again. This time for good.

Damn, maybe there's something in the water.

* * * *

All Stars Fall: A Seaside Pictures/Big Sky Novella
By Rachel Van Dyken

She *left*.

Two words I can't really get out of my head.

She left *us*.

Three more words that make it that much worse.

Three being another word I can't seem to wrap my mind around.

Three kids under the age of six, and she left because she missed it. Because her dream had never been to have a family, no, her dream had been to marry a rockstar and live the high life.

Moving my recording studio to Seaside Oregon seems like the best idea in the world right now especially since Seaside Oregon has turned into the place for celebrities to stay and raise families in between touring and producing. It would be lucrative to make the move, but I'm doing it for my kids because they need normal, they deserve normal. And me? Well, I just need a break and help, that too. I need a sitter and fast. Someone who won't flip me off when I ask them to sign an Iron Clad NDA, someone who won't sell our pictures to the press, and most of all? Someone who looks absolutely nothing like my ex-wife.

He's tall.

That was my first instinct when I saw the notorious Trevor Wood, drummer for the rock band Adrenaline, in the local coffee shop. He ordered a tall black coffee which made me smirk, and five minutes later I somehow agreed to interview for a nanny position. I couldn't help it; the smaller one had gum stuck in her hair while the eldest was standing on his feet and asking where babies came from. He looked so pathetic, so damn sexy and pathetic that rather than be star-struck, I took pity. I knew though; I knew the minute I signed that NDA, the minute our fingers brushed and my body became insanely aware of how close he was—I was in dangerous territory, I just didn't know how dangerous until it was too late. Until I fell for the star and realized that no matter how high they are in the sky—they're still human and fall just as hard.

* * * *

Envy: An Eagle Elite Novella
By Rachel Van Dyken

Every family has rules, the mafia just has more....
Do not speak to the bosses unless spoken to.
Do not make eye contact unless you want to die.
And above all else, do not fall in love.
Renee Cassani's future is set.
Her betrothal is set.
Her life, after nannying for the five families for the summer, is set.
Somebody should have told Vic Colezan that.
He's a man who doesn't take no for an answer.
And he only wants one thing.
Her.
Somebody should have told Renee that her bodyguard needed as much discipline as the kids she was nannying.
Good thing Vic has a firm hand.

About Rachel Van Dyken

Rachel Van Dyken is the *New York Times*, *Wall Street Journal*, and *USA TODAY* Bestselling author of regency and contemporary romances. When she's not writing you can find her drinking coffee at Starbucks and plotting her next book while watching The Bachelor.

She keeps her home in Idaho with her husband and adorable son. She loves to hear from readers!

For more information, visit her website at:
   http://rachelvandykenauthor.com

Discover 1001 Dark Nights

COLLECTION ONE
FOREVER WICKED by Shayla Black
CRIMSON TWILIGHT by Heather Graham
CAPTURED IN SURRENDER by Liliana Hart
SILENT BITE: A SCANGUARDS WEDDING by Tina Folsom
DUNGEON GAMES by Lexi Blake
AZAGOTH by Larissa Ione
NEED YOU NOW by Lisa Renee Jones
SHOW ME, BABY by Cherise Sinclair
ROPED IN by Lorelei James
TEMPTED BY MIDNIGHT by Lara Adrian
THE FLAME by Christopher Rice
CARESS OF DARKNESS by Julie Kenner

COLLECTION TWO
WICKED WOLF by Carrie Ann Ryan
WHEN IRISH EYES ARE HAUNTING by Heather Graham
EASY WITH YOU by Kristen Proby
MASTER OF FREEDOM by Cherise Sinclair
CARESS OF PLEASURE by Julie Kenner
ADORED by Lexi Blake
HADES by Larissa Ione
RAVAGED by Elisabeth Naughton
DREAM OF YOU by Jennifer L. Armentrout
STRIPPED DOWN by Lorelei James
RAGE/KILLIAN by Alexandra Ivy/Laura Wright
DRAGON KING by Donna Grant
PURE WICKED by Shayla Black
HARD AS STEEL by Laura Kaye
STROKE OF MIDNIGHT by Lara Adrian
ALL HALLOWS EVE by Heather Graham
KISS THE FLAME by Christopher Rice
DARING HER LOVE by Melissa Foster
TEASED by Rebecca Zanetti
THE PROMISE OF SURRENDER by Liliana Hart

COLLECTION THREE

HIDDEN INK by Carrie Ann Ryan
BLOOD ON THE BAYOU by Heather Graham
SEARCHING FOR MINE by Jennifer Probst
DANCE OF DESIRE by Christopher Rice
ROUGH RHYTHM by Tessa Bailey
DEVOTED by Lexi Blake
Z by Larissa Ione
FALLING UNDER YOU by Laurelin Paige
EASY FOR KEEPS by Kristen Proby
UNCHAINED by Elisabeth Naughton
HARD TO SERVE by Laura Kaye
DRAGON FEVER by Donna Grant
KAYDEN/SIMON by Alexandra Ivy/Laura Wright
STRUNG UP by Lorelei James
MIDNIGHT UNTAMED by Lara Adrian
TRICKED by Rebecca Zanetti
DIRTY WICKED by Shayla Black
THE ONLY ONE by Lauren Blakely
SWEET SURRENDER by Liliana Hart

COLLECTION FOUR

ROCK CHICK REAWAKENING by Kristen Ashley
ADORING INK by Carrie Ann Ryan
SWEET RIVALRY by K. Bromberg
SHADE'S LADY by Joanna Wylde
RAZR by Larissa Ione
ARRANGED by Lexi Blake
TANGLED by Rebecca Zanetti
HOLD ME by J. Kenner
SOMEHOW, SOME WAY by Jennifer Probst
TOO CLOSE TO CALL by Tessa Bailey
HUNTED by Elisabeth Naughton
EYES ON YOU by Laura Kaye
BLADE by Alexandra Ivy/Laura Wright
DRAGON BURN by Donna Grant
TRIPPED OUT by Lorelei James
STUD FINDER by Lauren Blakely
MIDNIGHT UNLEASHED by Lara Adrian

HALLOW BE THE HAUNT by Heather Graham
DIRTY FILTHY FIX by Laurelin Paige
THE BED MATE by Kendall Ryan
NIGHT GAMES by CD Reiss
NO RESERVATIONS by Kristen Proby
DAWN OF SURRENDER by Liliana Hart

COLLECTION FIVE
BLAZE ERUPTING by Rebecca Zanetti
ROUGH RIDE by Kristen Ashley
HAWKYN by Larissa Ione
RIDE DIRTY by Laura Kaye
ROME'S CHANCE by Joanna Wylde
THE MARRIAGE ARRANGEMENT by Jennifer Probst
SURRENDER by Elisabeth Naughton
INKED NIGHTS by Carrie Ann Ryan
ENVY by Rachel Van Dyken
PROTECTED by Lexi Blake
THE PRINCE by Jennifer L. Armentrout
PLEASE ME by J. Kenner
WOUND TIGHT by Lorelei James
STRONG by Kylie Scott
DRAGON NIGHT by Donna Grant
TEMPTING BROOKE by Kristen Proby
HAUNTED BE THE HOLIDAYS by Heather Graham
CONTROL by K. Bromberg
HUNKY HEARTBREAKER by Kendall Ryan
THE DARKEST CAPTIVE by Gena Showalter

COLLECTION SIX
DRAGON CLAIMED by Donna Grant
ASHES TO INK by Carrie Ann Ryan
ENSNARED by Elisabeth Naughton
EVERMORE by Corinne Michaels
VENGEANCE by Rebecca Zanetti
ELI'S TRIUMPH by Joanna Wylde
CIPHER by Larissa Ione
RESCUING MACIE by Susan Stoker
ENCHANTED by Lexi Blake

TAKE THE BRIDE by Carly Phillips
INDULGE ME by J. Kenner
THE KING by Jennifer L. Armentrout
QUIET MAN by Kristen Ashley
ABANDON by Rachel Van Dyken
THE OPEN DOOR by Laurelin Paige
CLOSER by Kylie Scott
SOMETHING JUST LIKE THIS by Jennifer Probst
BLOOD NIGHT by Heather Graham
TWIST OF FATE by Jill Shalvis
MORE THAN PLEASURE YOU by Shayla Black
WONDER WITH ME by Kristen Proby
THE DARKEST ASSASSIN by Gena Showalter

Discover Blue Box Press

TAME ME by J. Kenner
TEMPT ME by J. Kenner
DAMIEN by J. Kenner
TEASE ME by J. Kenner
REAPER by Larissa Ione
THE SURRENDER GATE by Christopher Rice
SERVICING THE TARGET by Cherise Sinclair

Ruthless Princess

Mafia Royals
By Rachel Van Dyken
Coming May 19, 2020

A mafia romance about best friends turned enemies by Rachel Van Dyken, the number one *New York Times* bestselling author of the Eagle Elite series.

The enemy of my enemy is my friend…

I never thought my father would ask this of me, to become the second generation at Eagle Elite University, to rule with an iron fist, and to take care of anyone who gets in our way.

But ever since the incident.

Ever since Him.

There's been a war in our little clique.

After all, a house divided cannot stand.

He's the problem, not me.

He used to kiss me like I was his oxygen.

Now he looks at me like I'm his poison.

But we both drank it, again and again, never believing there would be a day when our love would start a war.

And our friendship would shatter into a million pieces.

Then again, the worst thing you could do in the mafia is hang on to hope that your life will be normal.

The second worse thing?

Fall in love with your best friend.

Enemy.

And heir to the Nicolasi throne.

* * * *

"Welcome to day one!" Professor Dickface's eyes roamed around the room, purposefully scanning over us even though I had a middle finger raised in greeting right along with Serena, well at least we could agree on something, pissing off the professors enough to scare them shitless. "If you'll all log onto your blackboard app, we can go over this year's syllabus."

"Overjoyed," I said under my breath.

"Do you mind?" Serena hissed. "I'm learning here."

She literally had Snapchat open.

"Uh-huh." I elbowed her side only to feel the steel of a knife against my dick.

I kept my smirk in and lost when we both locked eyes.

Shit, I knew that look.

And I knew what typically followed.

The best sex of my life.

"No," I whispered hoarsely even though I let my eyes freely roam over her tight leather skirt down to gorgeous legs that I wanted to lick my way up. "Hell, no."

I jerked in my seat and nearly impaled myself on her knife when her hand slid across the front of my jeans.

I gritted my teeth to keep from reacting, braced my hands on the table in front of me and shook my head slowly as she kept touching, and I kept just reacting because it was Serena, and eons ago before she fucking broke my heart—she was mine.

"Choose me," I'd said in my head. "Choose me in front of them all!"

She didn't.

She never would.

Our love was impossible.

And I knew more than her—how easy love could start a war.

She still wasn't pulling her hand away, so I took matters into my own hands, and literally scooted my chair back, then slid my fingers up her thigh, digging into her skin the entire way up until I felt the string of her thong.

With a jerk, I tugged it until it broke, bunched her underwear in my hands, and then very somberly shoved them into my pocket all without looking away from my handy app.

"Give those back," she said through clenched teeth.

"Better not draw attention to us," I said in a bored tone. "Wouldn't want you to get detention on the first day—again."

"That was voluntary, and you know it!" She hissed.

I chuckled under my breath. "Whatever you say."

"Junior, I mean it! I can't walk around like this!"

"You can." I shrugged. "You will."

"Junior—"

"—Just admit defeat, you tried to win, and instead you just lost—embarrassingly. It's going to take more than your hand to get me off, or did you forget?" Then I did turn toward her. "I'd rather drink poison than have you touch me ever again."

Something sharp jabbed into my thigh. I winced and squeezed my eyes shut, then opened them and looked down.

And there was her knife, stuck in my thigh at least a half-inch past my jeans.

Perfect.

I nodded slowly. "Is that the Abandonato crest?"

"Beautiful, right?" She beamed then flipped her dyed golden hair in the air giving me a whiff of her cherry shampoo.

I jerked out the knife and handed it back to her. "Don't be creepy and lick the blood off—that's weird, even for you."

She just rolled her eyes. "More like using it in a spell to make your favorite appendage fall off."

"Your favorite appendage," I grumbled. "Remember? Oh God Junior, right there, so good, it's so—"

She clapped a hand over my mouth while a few students in front of us chuckled. "I get it, just. Stop. Talking."

I licked her hand and grinned.

She smiled and looked away, down at her phone. "It shouldn't be like this."

"I'll hate you for as long as we both shall live," I uttered the mantra we'd been repeating to each other for the last four years.

"Hate you," she repeated in a soft voice. "For as long as we both shall live."

And so the hurt continued.